THE VALENTINE

SHE'S ENJOYING A ROMANTIC MEAL. IT ISN'T
WITH ME.

MARIA FRANKLAND

AUTONOMY
PRESS

For my one and only Valentine, Michael
and a very happy wedding anniversary!

JOIN MY 'KEEP IN TOUCH' LIST

If you'd like to be kept in the loop about new books and special offers, join my 'keep in touch list' here or by visiting www.mariafrankland.co.uk

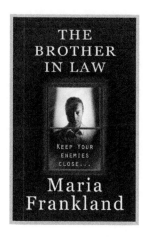

PROLOGUE

BLUE SWIRLING LIGHTS CUT through the mist as I get nearer to the pin on the map.

What the hell's going on? I know now what the saying *blood running cold* means. My blood feels frozen.

I park as near as I can get, abandoning the car where the crime scene tape has been stretched across the lane. I'm close enough to glimpse the chocolate box house, and, – I gasp in horror – the white tent that's been placed outside the porch.

I dart forward – after all, I've got every right. 'Oh my God – who is it? And what's happened?'

'Stand back, please.'

'But I might know— that could be my—'

'This is a crime scene.' An officer catches my arm and tugs me back. 'You can't go any further.'

'Please tell me what's going on. I think I know the—' My voice is drowned out as he cuts in again.

'Formal identification of the deceased will take place in the next few hours,' he says, his hand remaining on my arm. 'I know this must be difficult but if you could just let us get on with our jobs.'

'But—'

'Leave your contact details with me.' He pulls a notepad from his top pocket. 'I'll get the commanding officer to get in touch as soon as we've finished up here.' His tone tells me this isn't up for discussion.

A crime scene investigation van pulls up as I continue to watch on, needing to know who's inside that tent.

'You could at least tell me if it's a man or a woman.'

'I can't tell you anything. Not yet. I'm sorry.'

PART I

1

JUST BECAUSE IT'S dark doesn't mean I can't see across the street.

I'd recognise him anywhere. Tall, broad-chested and hunched. Always wearing shorts and walking boots, no matter what the weather.

The incessant rain has finally calmed to a chilly drizzle. The kind that makes you want to pull your curtains across the moment it becomes dark, and get cosy in front of your fire. But right now, I don't think there's anywhere I could get cosy. I shiver.

He's standing in his usual spot. In the shadow of the trees straight opposite my house. Is he trying to conceal himself or does he *want* me to know he's watching?

I fight the urge to grab my phone, to call my husband and shriek, *he's back – please hurry home*. I'd love for Dale to be at least a little concerned, especially *now* – for him to be compelled to rush back here, needing to protect me and our unborn child. But I know what he'd say with his usual bored expression... *It's all in your imagination, Tamara. The poor man's probably just waiting for someone.*

Yeah, *me*. Perhaps Dale will sit up and take notice when my body ends up in a shallow grave. The man stands there every night and it's always at the same time. He's never around when I initially arrive home. I get back from the salon at around half past six and Dale's normally an hour and a half later, after he's been to his precious gym. The man outside clearly knows our routine.

I glance at my little Fiat which I couldn't have parked any closer to the house. Each night before I pull in, I do a visual sweep of my garden. And then again before I get out of the car to make sure he isn't lying in wait to grab me as I dash to my porch. But it's always the same – he doesn't appear until I'm safely through the door.

I startle as my phone rings, hoping it's Dale. Perhaps he's somehow sensed my distress from his treadmill.

'Hi, Ali. You OK?' I can't keep the disgruntlement from my tone that it *isn't* my husband. I should have known better than to hope. He never calls me spontaneously anymore. The days when he used to call *just to hear my voice* feel like they happened in another lifetime.

'I could ask you the same question, sis.' She chuckles. 'You sound like you've just returned from a funeral.' Despite my disappointment, it's always a comfort to hear the familiarity of her voice. But I'm surprised that she's making any sort of joke about funerals – neither of us attended our father's twelve years ago and three years ago, I attended our mother's alone. The subject of our parents or any sort of death talk is usually off-limits between us. However, I've got other things to worry about right now.

'The bloody man's back. He's been there every night since the new year.' The heavy curtain falls back into position as I let it drop. I can't keep looking out into the street. Plus, who knows, my staring back at him might be giving him some sort of encouragement.

'I thought you were going to report him to the police.' She

6

sounds as beleaguered as Dale usually does. But just because neither of them has seen him doesn't mean it's all in my imagination.

'I *did* report him, actually. Last night.'

'When? You never mentioned it when we spoke.'

'It was later. Anyway, there was nothing much to mention – it was a complete waste of time.' I sigh at the memory as I sink into the armchair. 'He'd vanished by the time they got here.'

'Didn't they come straightaway?'

'No, it took them three hours – that's how important they thought it was. By then, Dale was moaning he was tired and wanted to go to bed.'

'Was he with you when they arrived?'

'Yeah – but he said while we were waiting that they'd probably do me for wasting police time. He reckons it's my hormones.'

Ali stays quiet, suggesting she probably agrees. What's got to happen for the two of them to take me seriously?

'They *did* look at me as though I might be unhinged.' I wince at the memory.

'So what did they say?'

'Well, I answered their questions. *What has he done? What has he said? How do you know it's you he's watching? Could he just be waiting for a lift?*'

'You mean, pretty much like I've been saying? Especially since you say he's out there at the same time each night.' She might be doing her best to disguise it, but Ali's voice is edged with irritation and something within me sags. If my sister isn't taking me seriously, what chance do I have of making anyone else listen?

'They told me they can't do anything against a man who's just *standing there* and instead, gave me a load of waffle about personal and house security. Then Dale made some barbed comment in front of them about *getting a life* and *finding some-*

thing better to do when I get home than staring through the window.'

A car, which sounds like Dale's, pulls up outside, so I spring back up from the chair. I've been like this a lot lately, and over the last couple of weeks, I've been getting worse. I can't sit still for more than a minute. And it's not just because of the man outside. My husband's budding friendship with one of our neighbours is also causing me concern.

'The police are kind of right, you know.' My sister's using the appeasing tone she always seems to reserve for me. '*If it's the same man out there every night, he could be there for any number of reasons.'*

'I'd just like to be more important than Dale's nightly visits to the bloody gym once in a while. He knows the upset this is causing for me.'

'I'm sure if you asked him, he'd have a night or two at home.'

'I've already tried.' I pace the rug, resisting the urge to return to my familiar spot at the window. 'There's nothing more important than his—.'

There's a huge shriek and a bang in Ali's background. 'Sorry, sis. Gotta go. It sounds like my two monsters might be killing each other. I'll call you back in a few minutes.'

Feeling lonelier than ever, I rest my phone on the coffee table, then unable to help myself, I return to the window and peel back the curtain, my gaze immediately darting to the spot where the man usually stands. I let a long breath out. He's gone.

The car I heard *was* Dale but for some reason, he hasn't pulled his car up behind mine on the drive. Instead, he's parked at the edge of the road outside our house.

His headlights fade as he reaches for his work bag from the passenger seat. I don't want him to see me looking out so I let the curtain drop. His car door bangs and my heart quickens as I wait for the sound of his footsteps to beat their path up the drive to our door.

But the night remains silent.

I peer around the edges of my curtain, hoping he won't spot me but already knowing what's likely to be causing his delay.

Yes, just as I suspected, Dale's talking to that woman across the road. He clearly enjoys her company far more than mine. She steps closer to him, touching his arm, looking to be hanging onto his every word. Now they're laughing together – he certainly never seems to laugh with *me* anymore. I know I've been miserable since becoming pregnant, not only with the sickness that is thankfully subsiding, but also with the fear that something's going to go wrong. This really isn't the time for him to withdraw – not when I need him the most.

The woman throws her head back, obviously loving every moment of their conversation. I can't believe *she's* the first person he wants to speak to upon arriving home after a long day away, instead of coming inside to start his evening with *me*. I bet he wishes he was going through her front door instead of returning to our side of the street.

And that's *definitely* what *she* wishes.

∿

Until the day I die, I'll marvel at your perfect face and the way you scrunch your face up when you're thinking.
I'll never take you for granted.

2

THE NEIGHBOUR'S house is lit up like a light show and as always, she hasn't closed her blinds. She usually doesn't until much later in the evening – it's as if she wants everyone to see inside her home, definitely an exhibitionist.

But I'm one to talk – I often nosy into her house from the vantage point of my darkened upstairs window. Naturally, her home is everything mine isn't. Hers is neutral, minimalist and feminine. In contrast, and just like our childhood home, mine's a mish-mash of colour and clutter. I'm like my mother was in that respect and no amount of reorganising and decluttering will ever alter that. Dale used to say he liked my style of living and that a house should look 'lived in.' However, these days, he moans like crazy about the lack of order in our surroundings. He'll have even more to complain about when the baby is born.

What the hell are they talking about? She's all over him, yet, she barely gives me the time of day whenever I say hello. I'm lucky to get a curt nod as I'm coming and going from the house.

I jump as my phone bursts back into life and snatch it up from the table. I'm so on edge. I rest a protective hand over my still-flat belly. All this stress can't be any good for the baby.

'It's me again. I've managed to avert World War Three between the terrors.' My sister laughs. 'Anyway, the reason I was ringing in the first place was to check you're still OK to babysit these little darlings on Saturday. You haven't forgotten, have you?'

'Of course not.' Something brightens inside me. I adore my nephews and love my auntie time. I've already got our movie evening and treats planned. The only spanner in the works is that Dale and I will be apart overnight. I've suggested so many times that we babysit together but he never wants to.

'It's just I know you've got a lot on your mind, and—'

'It's fine, honestly – you can ask whenever you need to. You know how much I love being around them.'

'Ah good.' I can hear the relief in her voice. 'They can't wait. You'd think they hadn't seen you for a month, not just a week.'

'Anyway...' Yet again, I peer around the edge of the curtain. 'He's gone.'

'Who's gone?'

'The man.'

'Oh, *that* man. See, what did I tell you – his lift has probably arrived. But you need to stop looking out of your window all the time, Tamara. You'll drive yourself bananas.'

'It's not just out of *this* window. He was hanging around near the salon last week and he was even standing two places behind me in the checkout queue at the weekend.' I'm still unnerved by the memory. I've never run to my car so fast with a shopping trolley.

'For goodness sake, he's allowed to do his shopping. It'll just be a coincidence that you've seen him near the salon. Otley's not exactly a vast place in which to live.'

'It's the way he looks at me – I've got a really bad feeling.'

'You've *always* had an overactive imagination,' she chuckles. 'In fact, you're far worse now than when we were kids.'

First funerals, now childhood. Like the topic of our parents, the subject of our childhood usually stays dead and buried. However, I have to admit that impending motherhood is drawing bad memories and long-pushed-down feelings of guilt back to the surface. And I don't have the same energy as I had pre-pregnancy to keep squashing them down. But somehow, I must keep my focus on the present.

'Honestly Ali, you're as dismissive as Dale. And speaking of him, he's over the road with that bloody neighbour of ours again.' I fling myself into the armchair. It's better than continuing to watch them as I drive myself insane.

'*Which* neighbour?'

'The one I told you about the other week. Gosh, do you *ever* listen to me? You know, the one with perfect blonde hair, eyes that are too big for her face and legs up to her armpits.'

'She doesn't sound all that great.' Ali laughs. 'She sounds like one of the Mr Men.'

Another reference to our childhood. My father bought us all those books. It's one of the rare decent memories I have of him.

'Well, Dale seems pretty taken by her.'

'He's probably just being neighbourly.'

'Every single night this week, they've been out there when he's got home from work, laughing and chatting. How would you feel if it was Wayne?'

She doesn't reply. She doesn't need to. We both know how much Wayne dotes on her. He can't get home from work fast enough each night to return to Ali and the boys. Meanwhile, I've married someone who's as emotionally available as my parents always were.

'You make it sound like they're jumping into bed together, Tamara. They're only *talking*.'

'That's where it all starts.'

'You're being paranoid, sis. Look I've been there – hormones are funny—'

'It's not my hormones.' The words slip through my gritted teeth. 'I really think something is going on.'

I glance at the wall, my eyes resting on our wedding photo. We've been married for fourteen years and any magic we once had seems to have evaporated ages ago, certainly for Dale. I'd do anything to recapture it. I'm just praying that the baby's born safely this time and will cement us back together. I keep telling myself that my pregnancy is the catalyst for his recent withdrawal. That he's wary of becoming too attached to the baby after all the loss we've previously suffered. I'd like to talk about all this with my sister but to raise it risks tempting fate. I can't lose this baby. I've come too far this time.

I've been counting the days down until tomorrow. Valentine's Day.

3

'You need to get a grip, sis. For the baby's sake, if not your own.'

'That's easy for you to say.' I rise back from my chair. I *need* to see what's going on out there. I can't imagine how they've got so much to discuss. 'Your hubby's besotted with you.' My mood plummets even further. 'You'll no doubt have a lovely Valentine's card and a dozen red roses waiting for you in the morning.' In the job I do, it's impossible to forget what day it is tomorrow.

Ali laughs. 'It's all a load of commercial nonsense really – Valentine's Day, I mean. You get far too hung up on stuff like that. I mean, it's nice to get something, but it's all just a money-making ploy.'

'You'd be *hung up* if *you* didn't get anything from Wayne.' My eyes flit back over the road again. She's resting her hand on his arm now. I should probably march over there and demand to know what's going on. *How dare they carry on like this right under my nose? What the hell are they talking about?* I wonder if she knows I'm pregnant. Maybe if I told her, she'd back off.

'You should have a proper chat with Dale if you're this

unhappy. You can't go on like this – you're going to make your-self ill.'

'I already feel sick to the stomach.'

'I thought the sickness was easing.'

'It's not just the pregnancy – it's my nerves too – I just can't seem to relax.'

'Oh, Tamara.'

'Look, I *know* that man's hanging around out there and watching me, but no one, not even the police seem bothered. And I *know* that bloody neighbour's after my husband. From what I'm seeing out there, he fancies her right back as well.' There, I've said it out loud and it certainly hasn't made me feel any better.

'You need to speak to him. Life's far too short to be miserable in your marriage.'

'They say you marry someone like your father. And I really have, haven't I?'

'You're mentioning *him* a lot lately,' Ali says.

'It's *you* who made him a taboo subject after he died.'

'*After he died*,' she echoes. 'You make it sound like it was a gentle death.'

As if we're going down this road.

'Do you think you should go for more counselling, sis?' She continues. 'Becoming a parent can bring all sorts of shit up about your own childhood. Believe me, I know.'

'I've got enough to worry about without raking up the past. And I can only hope I do a better job of being a parent than *he* did.'

'You'll be wonderful.' Her voice relaxes. 'Wayne and I can't wait to become auntie and uncle.'

I turn my attention back to the street. The light from the streetlamp illuminates the woman's blonde head, casting a halo of light. She must sense me watching as suddenly, though it's impossible to tell in the darkness, she seems to be looking across. Then Dale looks too. 'Shit.' I let the curtain fall. 'I think they've seen me watching.'

'Are they *still* talking?'

'Yeah. Do you think I should have it out with him?'

'It sounds like you should – you need to have your mind put at rest. But remember, it's *you* he comes home to every night, Tamara.'

'He's done it before, so he can do it again, can't he?' I stare at the pattern on the carpet – the carpet we chose when we moved in here six months ago. We spent a ton of time together for a couple of months getting the house sorted, no doubt to assuage his guilty conscience. But now that he's got me back where he wants me, he's off again. Back into his usual ways.

'I thought you'd managed to get beyond his affair. Especially now, with the baby.'

'I don't think I ever can.'

Ali sighs. 'I always said you should go for marriage counselling. Relationships *can* be stronger after an affair but you've got to do the work.'

'I didn't do anything wrong – *he's* the one who made a mockery of our wedding vows. For *eight* months.' I close my eyes at the memory of the day I found him in *our* bed with his colleague at our last house.

He ricocheted between me and her for a couple more months until she kicked Dale to the kerb, and chose to stay with her husband. I'd wanted him to have *chosen* to stay with me, instead of the other woman having done the choosing. I was so close to leaving him forever and went to stay with Ali while I worked out a plan. But then Dale lured me back with his promises of another try at IVF and a house move to somewhere nearer my work.

'I thought you'd forgiven him.' My sister's voice is soft. 'The house you're in, wasn't it supposed to be a complete new start?'

Tears fill my eyes for what must be the millionth time today.

I'm all over the place at the moment. No wonder he's avoiding me and preferring to spend his time talking to Miss Perfect over the road.

'I hate to be an *I-told-you-so* but I still think it was daft to have a baby with someone you can't trust.'

She knows as well as I do that I'm getting to my 'last chance saloon' on so many levels. The final frozen embryos and my age are conspiring against me. When I add this truth to the other bitter, self-deprecating realisations that are already swimming around inside me, it's no wonder I'm so miserable and anxious. No amount of counselling could help me right now. The one and only person who could make me feel better is my husband. If only I could feel secure with him like I did for our first few years together, instead of always worrying that he's planning to run out on our marriage. But perhaps this is all I deserve.

'Listen to me, Tamara – you can't go on like this. You're saying the same things to me about your marriage *every* time we speak. I'm really worried about the amount of stress you're piling onto yourself.'

'I'm sorry – you must be getting so sick of me.'

'Of course, I'm not. But you don't need me to tell you that things have to change.'

'If only it were that simple.'

'You haven't dealt with Dale's affair properly, either of you – that's what I think. You've swept it under the carpet just like...' Her voice trails off, though I can imagine what she was going to say. She was going to liken me to Mum but has clearly managed to stop herself.

'If the two of you don't do something about it soon, it's going to completely rot your relationship. Do you want to bring your baby into that kind of atmosphere?'

I'm heartened by the fact that she's referring to the baby in forthcoming and tangible terms. Until my scan came and went, we were all too frightened to countenance that this time, the pregnancy really might progress. We all wept when we saw the heartbeat, me, Ali and even Dale. It still feels like an absolute miracle.

'I know what you're saying, but Dale won't even *consider* counselling. Every time I mention it, he gives me the silent treatment for the rest of the evening.'

'I think counselling could be your magic bullet. Dale would be forced to listen and to face up to how much he's hurt you.'

'How he continues to hurt me.'

'Don't you want more out of life for yourself?' Fresh tears leap to my eyes at my sister's words. She always manages to hit the bullseye. 'Take the baby out of the equation for the moment. You deserve to be happy and you're a million miles away from that.'

'Do I?'

'Of course you do. You should be *living*, rather than just existing?'

'I *am* living. It's just—'

'Give over, Tamara,' she says. 'You know as well as I do that something badly needs to change.'

Tomorrow, I'm going to show you just how much you mean to me.

4

FINALLY, Dale's key twists in the lock and the front door bangs. My heart rate increases so fast that I wish I could settle myself down with a glass of wine. What I wouldn't give for one.

'What's for dinner?' My husband ducks under the door-frame as though nothing's wrong and dumps his bag on the island before pecking me on the forehead. I've no idea when this started – when he began to kiss the top of my head instead of wrapping me in his arms and planting a kiss on my lips. He used to tell me he'd missed me, but he never does these days. If he *did* miss me, he wouldn't have been hanging around out there with her for over twenty minutes.

'I haven't got a clue.' That's all he cares about. His dinner. Not me and the upset he's caused, nor the baby. No, he just cares about what I might have already cooked that could have been ruined while he was so busy talking to *her*. As I drove home earlier, I was mentally planning what to cook. Stir fry or salmon, I was thinking. But my insides are so knotted around each other, I could no longer eat a thing.

'What's the matter? Is everything OK?' He points at my

belly. I can hardly wait until the pregnancy shows and I can begin wearing maternity clothes. Perhaps he'll love me more then. After all, he wants to become a daddy just as much as I want to become a mummy. We've waited for so long for this and I'm certain that the baby will be the tie which finally binds us.

'The man was back out there earlier.' Any minute Dale will tell me to stop tapping my foot against my chair. I can't believe how antsy I am tonight. I can't seem to sit still.

'Oh for goodness sake, Tamara.' He shakes his head and his brow furrows. 'Like the police said last night, just because a bloke's waiting at the other side of the street, it doesn't mean he's looking at *you*.' He plucks a glass from the cupboard.

'How come you're drinking on a school night?' I point at it.

'You're just jealous because you can't have one with me.' He grins. 'Actually, it's been a long day.'

'Twenty minutes longer than it should have been.' Feeling queasy with nerves, I fill a glass with water.

'What do you mean?'

I jerk my head in the direction of the front of the house as he walks back towards me. 'I saw you again, out there with *her*.'

'You mean Rachel? Oh, we were only having a laugh about something.' He grabs the neck of the wine bottle and I can picture myself doing the same with *her* scrawny neck.

'So you know her name now? Well, this is great, this is.'

'I was chatting to our bloody neighbour, that's all.' His voice takes on an appeasing edge. 'Anyway, I thought you were over all that jealousy.'

I want to remind him he's only got himself to blame for evoking my jealousy in the first place after his previous behaviour, but I won't ruin our evening any more than it already has been. I'm stressed enough without us having a row. No, I'll stay calm but I do want to get to the bottom of things. My sister was right before, I can't keep going on like this. Life *is* too short to be unhappy.

'So what were you laughing about?'

'My shoddy parking if you must know.' Dale's eyes crinkle in the corners as he smiles. 'She's actually a nice woman, you ought to try speaking to her yourself.'

'I have.' My voice is a growl. I'm not going to tell him how many times I've tried; I don't want to make myself look any more stupid. As soon as I clapped eyes on her I had a bad feeling and decided straightaway to befriend her. There's the saying, *keep your friends close and your enemies closer* but it hasn't quite worked out like that. 'She doesn't give *me* the time of day.'

'Have you looked in a mirror lately, love?' Dale's tone is still pleasant as he gestures to my make-up mirror which I keep on the windowsill for doing my brows in a decent light. Oh great, here comes another put-down. Hopefully, it won't be as cutting as the remarks Dad used to dish out to Mum to keep her in her place such as, *what's up, have you forgotten your HRT again?* Or his other favourite, *at least you were pretty and slim once.* 'That permanent scowl on your face,' Dale continues, 'and everlasting hunch of your shoulders doesn't exactly invite people to be warm and friendly towards you, does it?'

I'm not having this. How dare he turn the tables? *He's* had the affairs. *He's* the one who puts off returning home for as long as possible, and *he's* the one who's out there, enjoying chatting and laughing with his new neighbour more than his wife.

'We need to talk, Dale.' I tug a chair from under the island and try not to look at the glass of wine he's poured. A bit of Dutch courage would do me the world of good.

'What, right at this moment? I've only just walked into the house.'

'There's no time like the present, is there? Then we've got the rest of the evening to actually get along.'

'This sounds ominous.' He hangs his jacket on the back of another chair and sits facing me. 'Here we go again.'

If you were mine, you'd want for nothing.

5

'No, it's not *here we go again*.' I press my fingers together as though saying a silent prayer. 'Do I need to remind you who did all the damage to our marriage in the first place? It wasn't me who—'

'I've told you I'm sorry until I'm purple in the face,' he cuts in, his face darkening. 'You said I was forgiven.'

'Forgiven *maybe*, but I'll never forget. How can I when you're out there every evening, flirting with our neighbour right under my nose.'

'It's not *every* night. And we're *not* flirting. Well, *I'm* not flirting.'

'But *she* is, is that what you're saying?' I knew it. She's probably one of those who enjoys the challenge of the unavailable. Looking at her, she could have any man she wants, so she's not going to let the small matter of someone being married stop her from helping herself to someone else's husband. And she probably doesn't even know I'm pregnant. I can't imagine Dale will have enlightened her.

'No, that's not what I'm saying.' He takes a large sip of his wine and loosens his tie. His dark hair is becoming flecked with grey where it frames his face, just like his father's was. He's such a good-looking man and at nearly forty, he's getting better with age. Unlike me. The fact I've been labelled as a geriatric pregnancy on my maternity notes *and* referred to as such in front of all the whippersnapper midwifery students was not helpful. 'Look, we really can't go on like this.'

His words echo exactly what my sister said on the phone earlier. 'I know we can't. But you won't change, will you? You know how insecure I am, yet you won't do or say anything to help me feel better.'

'You know I don't go in for all this needy behaviour. It's an absolute turn-off.'

'Everything about me seems to be a turn-off.'

'That's not true at all, but really, love, no one wants to be around a whining, insecure nag – you must already know that.'

I do, deep down, and I know nonchalance would be a better course of action but I can't seem to help myself. When Dale was flitting between me and his former colleague early last year, the loneliness when I knew he was with *her* was like being stabbed in the heart. Not to mention the confidence crash I suffered. I still believe if she hadn't returned to her husband, Dale would still be with her rather than with me. And there'd be no baby.

'I'm not *choosing* to feel like this – I'd give my right arm for us to be happily married again – and to just be looking forward to the baby.'

'It's *you* that's preventing us from being happy, love.' His voice is soft, as though he's chastising a child. This is *not* my fault but he always manages to make me feel like it is.

'Ali reckons we should go for counselling before the baby's born. She thinks it will help.'

'So you've been spouting off about me *again* to your sister?'

'I've got to talk to *someone*?' The tears are threatening to spill. I won't cry, I can't cry. Just as my father did, Dale views crying as a sign of weakness and avoids me like the plague when I succumb. He doesn't know how to deal with it.

'You're talking to *me*, now, aren't you?' He says. I feel like a specimen under his microscope as he curls his fingers around the stalk of his wine glass while not taking his eyes off me. I remember when he used to look at me with love and longing in his eyes.

'The two of us need to talk, Dale, *properly*. I think Ali's right – we *do* need to get together with a counsellor if we're going to save our marriage.' I'm not going to tell him how badly I want us to save our marriage. Not with what he's just said about me being needy.

'Are things *that* bad?'

'For me they are. I can't trust you. After everything that's happened, you should be pulling out all the stops to reassure me, not blaming me for being insecure.'

'I can't keep paying for my mistakes forever,' Dale snaps and my insides contract. I've got to make things better. According to my pregnancy book, at thirteen weeks gestation, the baby is now able to hear things. I don't want it being born as anxious as I am. Plus, if things get much worse between us this evening, I risk Dale storming out of here and heading to the pub. Or worse, I risk driving him straight across the road to *Rachel*.

'No, but you *keep* making the mistakes, don't you?' I try to lower my voice. 'Look, I'm sorry.' This is escalating into a row, just as I feared. I've got to try and pull things back. 'Why don't we do something nice together tomorrow? We could get dressed up and stay overnight at a hotel. Let's try and recapture some of what we once had.'

His expression is a cross between saying, *what did we have?* and *no chance.*

'I'm sorry, love, but I have to work later than normal tomorrow.'

'But it's Valentine's Day.'

'Oh, come on, we don't go in for all that rubbish. It's just businesses trying to make more money out of gullible idiots.'

'You've changed so much, Dale. I'll never forget you sending me roses on Valentine's Day, do you remember – the first year we moved in together?'

'I was trying to impress you.' His previous irritated face thankfully relaxes into a grin. 'But I've got no need to now, have I?'

'No, you're too busy going out and trying to impress every bugger else instead.' I slam my glass down so hard, it's a miracle it doesn't break. I can't help myself. How dare he sit there and say he's got no need to try with me anymore? Is this what it's always going to be like?

His grin fades. 'It's getting to the point where I'm dreading coming home to you,' he snaps. 'Is this what you want for us? For the baby?'

'At least you're being honest with me now.' I drain the last of my water. 'Which is why you'd rather talk to her across the road than your own wife.'

'No one could blame me,' he snaps. Then he glances towards the cooker. 'So I guess it's a takeaway then?'

'Sort yourself out. I'm not hungry.'

~

If you were mine,
I'd cook for you morning, noon and night.

26

6

I'VE NEVER SLEPT WELL since Dale stopped wrapping his arms around me as we fall asleep. I've tried to blame it on the fact that we often come to bed at different times, but really, it's just another thing that's gone pear-shaped in our marriage – another distance between us. I can't pinpoint when he stopped kissing me on the lips upon leaving and returning to the house, nor when we started sleeping back to back in our huge bed. I stare at the muscular curve of his shoulder. If he gets much closer to the edge of his side of the bed, I swear he'll fall on the floor. I lay my palm against my belly. I'm carrying his child. We should be closer than ever. Yet we're as far apart as a pair of bookends.

Blinking back the threat of tears, I roll onto my back and stare into the darkness. I knew every shape and trick of the light in our old house but this one's still unfamiliar and I've never quite settled. Dale's rhythmic breathing used to lull me to sleep but tonight, it's plain irritating. I reach for my phone. Perhaps if I try to read, that might tire my eyes. Instead, I find myself opening Facebook. I'll probably drive myself mad looking at the perfect lives of others but I'm drawn to it like a drug. Ali would tell me I enjoy making myself miserable. Tomorrow will be hard – my Facebook feed will be full of the romantic declarations of others and people bragging about how they're spending Valentine's Day. So I'll stay well away from social media until the public displays of affection are well and truly over. If only I didn't have to go to work.

Dale Fenton has been tagged in a post.

He never told me he'd been out for lunch with his colleagues from his new job. I wonder if it was planned. Was he more dressed up when he left for work this morning? My eyes are immediately drawn to the women sitting around the pub table with him, especially the younger and prettier women. One of them I recognise from his Christmas party, but two of them I've never met. For a split second, I want to wake him up and ask why he never mentioned going out to me when he got home. What else has he got to hide?

Rachel Moorhouse has commented. Something twists in my belly. It's her from over the road.

Not only has she 'hearted' the post, she's also written on it, *Looking good, Dale. xxx*

They're bloody Facebook friends. I don't believe it. How dare she post on his page like this when she knows full well he's married? And with three kisses? I stare at his image on my screen until his face blurs. His piercing blue eyes and vibrant smile have always caused people to take notice of him but up until eighteen months ago, I thought I'd won back his sole attention. Until everything went as sour as it was the first time. And now for the third time, it looks as though it's all going wrong again.

I stare at his outline in the darkness. I'm absolutely gutted. I've risked so much and put so much on the line for this man that if I don't get away from him sharpish, I'm going to end up elbowing him in the ribs and demanding to know why he's Facebook friends with Rachel bloody Moorhouse and why she feels like she's got the right to tell him he's *looking good*. I swing my legs out of bed and reach for my dressing gown. I need to work out how the hell I'm going to handle this without driving him completely away. I can't bring a baby into the world all on my own – I don't want to be a single mother. I have to make things happy. I have to lure him back.

Bitch. Bitch. Bitch. As I reach the hallway, I tug the curtain over the window to one side and stare out into the night. She's closed her blinds and her house is now in darkness. As are most of the other houses along the street.

My attention averts to a movement to the left of her house. Oh my God, it's *him* – the man! It's nearly midnight and he's right there again, straight opposite my home. I blink, just in case my weary eyes are playing tricks.

They're not.

I reach into my pocket for my phone. This time, I'm going to get a photo. It'll be time-stamped, therefore the police will be *forced* to act on it when they arrive. Perhaps they'll circulate it in the news – or maybe I should take matters into my own hands? Post it on the local Otley, Our Town Facebook group and see if anybody recognises him. It's not normal behaviour – to stand outside someone's house when it's pushing towards midnight, just watching.

With fumbling fingers, I get through my phone's lock screen and open the camera. I need to remember what to do with the brightness and flash settings to get a reasonable picture in the dark. But by the time I point it through the window and in the man's direction, he's vanished.

I'm struggling to get my breath. If I try calling the police at this time of the night when he's not even there, it will just reinforce their belief that I'm an over-imaginative mad woman. I rub my eyes again. Maybe I am. After all, it's dark out there and he can't have just been there one minute, gone the next. I've been in the salon earlier and earlier each morning, especially this week while there's been the demand for Valentine's manicures. Plus I've been all over the place with my sleep. And then there's my hormones. So for now, I'll do nothing. I'll make some chamomile tea and try and get warm and comfy on the sofa. Tomorrow, I've got a mad busy day. I need to get some rest and I have more chance of getting a few hours sleep down here on my own than beside my husband. After all, he can hardly bear to be anywhere near me these days.

Whenever I watch you, I have the urge to wrap you in my arms and show you just how much I love you.

7

I JUMP at the shriek of my alarm with a crick in my neck and a cramp in my shin. Thumping at my phone to silence it, I rise to sit and massage my leg. Memories of last night hit me like a sledgehammer and no doubt, as always, it's going to fall on me to make amends. So, I'm going to apologise to Dale for last night, and hopefully, the cheeky Valentine's card I've bought him will set the tone for a better day. Perhaps he'll even agree to us going out together for a drink, even if it's only for an hour after his late finish.

'Dale?' My voice echoes around the silent room.

I stagger to the door, hoping the movement will bring some life back into my cramped leg. I pause at the bottom of the stairs.

'Dale? Are you awake?'

I tilt my watch – it's just before eight. 'You'd better get a move on or you'll be late.' And so had I. I guess it's not the end of the world if the girls arrive at the salon before me – they've both got a key. However, as the shop's owner, I like to set a positive example. Plus, Valentine's Day is as busy as Christmas Eve.

I wait for a moment, still expecting him to appear at the top of the stairs, with his hair on end, asking why I've been down-stairs all night and moaning that I've let him oversleep. But he doesn't.

I take the stairs two at a time to find nothing but the woody scent of his aftershave lingering in our room and the foam from his shower gel in the ensuite. He's even made the bed – could it be a guilty conscience? I wrench the curtains apart – there's just a dry patch on the road where his car's been parked overnight and Rachel opposite, has, as always, opened all her blinds and allowed a full view into her home by turning on her lights. The two of them have probably been standing here, waving to each other while I've been crunched up on the sofa, oblivious.

The man who's been standing on the street gawping into *my* house would have a far better view if instead, he were to gawp into Rachel's. Plus, she's a hundred times prettier than me. My puffy and bloodshot eyes stare back at me from the mirror in my wardrobe door. I look at least ten years older than my thirty-seven years this morning and I've lost weight at a time when I should be gaining it. I look like my mother. That's a thought I need to shake from my mind. Clearly, I just need to get myself ready and amongst other people. I've been on my own for too long. Ali was right, I'm driving myself insane with my unhappy thoughts.

The red envelope poking from the drawer of my dressing table makes me feel even more miserable. Maybe I should have left Dale's card out for him to find. Perhaps he'd have felt guilty and woken me with a cup of tea and a kiss, instead of sneaking out of the house without a word. It was around this time last year when I discovered his last affair. Prior to that, whilst he might have thought all the Valentine's stuff was hyped-up commercialism, he still made the effort each year to buy me flowers and write me a card. He should love me even more now I'm carrying his baby, and this time it looks like I'll be carrying it successfully. Instead, he seems to love me less.

Thankfully, I never have to think about what I'm wearing when I'm getting ready for work. I slide a pair of fitted black leggings from the shelf and one of my purple *Beauty by Tamara* tunics from a hanger. It all still fits me at the moment, but I look forward to when my bump finally emerges and I have to buy a maternity tunic.

I can't go to work looking this bad. My first appointment isn't until half-past nine so there's time for some urgent rectification for my face and hair, even if it means I won't be first at the salon. It won't do for a beauty therapist to look anything other than fresh-faced and dewy-eyed. I couldn't look any less fresh-faced and dewy-eyed. It's *me* who could do with a day of pampering. What I wouldn't give to have a top-to-toe massage and a relaxing facial in a candlelit room.

As I push open the door into the kitchen, I still find myself hoping against all hope that Dale's left me *something* for Valentine's Day, even if it's just a card propped up against the plant pot on the island, where he usually leaves cards or notes. He used to leave lovely notes for me all over the place in our early days of living together – even in my packed lunch. But there's nothing, Absolutely nothing.

I stare at the remnants from the takeaway he ordered last night as I force down some toast. He moans about clutter yet leaves his own everywhere.

I sip my tea, beginning to feel slightly more human. I wish I hadn't gone off coffee as I've got such a long day. I could do with more energy than tea will provide.

Dale drank nearly an entire bottle of wine last night and the evening became increasingly strained. While I tried and failed to focus on the novel I've had on the go since the new year, I kept looking over at him. As always, he was scrolling and messaging on his phone. This was clearly more appealing than talking to his wife. And now, after that Facebook post, I can't help but worry he was messaging the woman across the road.

It's less than a year since Dale's last affair ended and already, it looks like he's begun another one.

I love to look at you, I'd love even more to run my fingers through your hair and tell you how amazing you are.

8

As I pull the door behind me, I have the familiar prickle down the back of my neck of being watched. I can't stand this for much longer – it's like being violated from the outside in and makes me feel sweaty and nauseous. This is no good for the baby, no good at all.

I rest my hand on my belly as I sweep my gaze up and down the street, expecting to see the tall, stocky man in shorts and a hooded coat, but instead, I lock eyes with Rachel. It's difficult to see her expression at this distance but if I were to hazard a guess, it would be somewhere between pure condescension and hatred.

Then, as if I'm nothing to her, she continues to put her bags onto her back seat. It's no good – I'll *have* to say something to persuade her to back off from my husband. She'll probably go bleating to him, telling tales. But whatever I do or say, it's not as if I'll make things any worse. Unless Dale leaves me, things *can't* get any worse than they were last night.

'What's with the Facebook messages to *my* husband?' I call to her as I march to the end of my drive.

'Eh? What?' She stands up straight from her car and looks at me as though she can't believe I have the nerve to directly address her.

'You heard.' I stride across the street. 'Telling him *he's looking good*? What game do you think you're playing?'

'You'll drive him away with that jealousy of yours, Tamara.' She gives me a knowing look. 'You ought to be careful.'

She's even prettier closer up than from the distance across the street I've frequently observed her from. Shiny hair, even shinier eyes and yes, a perfect dewy complexion. She'd be the perfect advert for my business and I'm no match for her.

'How do you know my name?' My voice hardens. 'What's he said to you?'

'Dear me.' She shakes her head before gesturing to the embroidered name on my tunic. 'You need to get a grip. Now, if you'll excuse me.' She opens her car door, leaving me seething as I stand on the footpath, watching her slide her perfect self, all pencil skirt and shapely legs, into her car. Suddenly, I'm even more consumed with rage.

I march to the driver's side and bang on the window. How dare she dismiss me so callously?

'You're making me late for work.' She opens her door a fraction.

'Has he told you I'm three months pregnant? Our baby's due at the end of the summer.'

'Really, I couldn't care less.' She slams her door.

I'm shaking as she reverses past me. To use the expression she just has, I really *have* got to get a grip. My baby needs me to be on an even keel, not swinging between extremes of anxiety and anger. I should just get myself to work and within a couple of hours, I'll be distracted. But as I turn to head back over to my side of the road, my attention's averted to her windowsill. She's displayed a huge card beside a vase of red roses. If I were to count them, I know there'd be a dozen. The sick feeling in the pit of my belly intensifies. What if they've been bought by *my* husband?

I stamp back to my drive, cursing her with every step. And him. Dale and I have no chance of getting back on track with her doing everything she can to sink her claws into him. I really don't know what to do.

Or perhaps, I do. No matter how hard this is going to be, I've got to take action before it's too late.

My sister's words swim back into my mind after yesterday's phone conversation.

Life's too short to be stuck in an unhappy marriage.

I let myself back into the house and head straight to the kitchen. It's always the first room Dale goes to when he arrives home, especially on a Friday when he wants to pour himself a drink. I can be sure he'll see what I'm about to write for him straight away.

Temporarily leaving him is what worked for me last time. My taking myself off for a few days last March, was, as he said, what brought him to his senses. Rachel might be all curves and doe eyes but it's *me* with whom Dale has the history. You can't be with someone since your teenage years and not know each other inside out and back to front. And it's *me* who's about to make him a father.

He had no idea where I was when I stayed at my sister's as she was more than willing to cover for me and being unable to reach me made him pine.

'It's made me realise how much I still love you,' he said as he took both my hands in his. 'I badly want us to work things out.'

I can make him feel this way again. Can't I?

Or could it force him even closer to *her*?

~

It's finally here.
The day when everything changes.

9

PERHAPS I NEED to give myself more time to weigh up what I'm planning. The more I think about it, the more worried I feel that my clearing off will just give Rachel exactly what she's been waiting for – my husband on a silver platter. Maybe hoping he'll chase after me again is stupid.

If only I knew what to do for the best. Stay here and fight for our marriage or leave for a few days and risk losing him forever. Even leaving just *temporarily* could be long enough for him to hotfoot it over to Rachel's and forget all about my existence. It's a gamble, but is it one I'm willing to lose?

Then a memory of his face when he found me after five days last year slips into my mind. His anguish coupled with relief. Maybe I'll tell him I'm going for a matter of days rather than permanently. If he thinks I'm not coming back, *ever*, who knows what could happen between him and that cow over the road?

My gaze roams over our beautiful new kitchen. This house was supposed to be a fresh start for us, but all I've done is jump out of the frying pan and into the fire. I grab a pen from the pot. This is no time to continue being indecisive. It's time for action.

Going away for a few days. Not sure when I'll be back. Need to get my head straight and work out whether I still want to be married. Don't know what I want anymore. I don't think you do either.

It's a similar note to what I left last year and it might be a cliche but absence nearly always makes the heart grow fonder. At least I hope it will. I'm always here at home at the same time as Dale, so being away should allow him the opportunity to miss me. Maybe I could leave his Valentine's card here too? That might make him feel worse.

What an idiot I am. Of course I shouldn't. He's walked out of the house without a single word to me this morning. So as tough as it's going to be, I *have* to go through with my plan. Some space between us is the only chance of bringing him to his senses. I've tried everything else to get through to him lately and it's not just my own happiness that's at stake. I've now got the baby to consider.

Pulling the door behind me, I breathe in the February chill as I lock up. It's time to paint on my false smile and adopt my bright and breezy persona for work. Being a beauty therapist – especially as it's *my* own business – is like being on stage all day, every day. I have to present my best self and be interested in the lives and loves of all my customers, even when I'm having a bad day. And I've had a lot of those over the last few weeks.

I throw my handbag and overnight bag into the boot and head to the driver's side. I haven't a clue where I'm going to stay tonight but at lunchtime, I'll jump on Booking.com and find somewhere that can double up as a treat. I can't go too far as I'm taking care of my nephews tomorrow night. I'll find somewhere self-contained where Ali can drop them off to stay with me, rather than going to her house again. Hers would be the first place Dale would look, and after last time, he wouldn't believe her if she were to say I was somewhere else. Other women will be getting treated to weekend breaks for Valentine's Day so why shouldn't I have the same? Anyway, once I've covered or shifted tomorrow's appointments, we're closed on Sunday and Monday. I'll probably stay away for the entire three days. That should *really* get him wondering where I've gone.

Dale's often berated me for never carrying out any maintenance checks on my car and always leaving things like air, oil and water for him to monitor. He claims to always give his car a visual once-over every time before he drives.

But I don't, and it's not until I've nearly backed the Fiat from our drive that I realise something's amiss. It's the grind of metal – the rims of my wheels against the concrete of the drive that makes me stop. I pull the handbrake on, and jump out to check around the car.

I don't believe this. All four of my tyres have been slashed.

The street's silent except for the postman who's around ten doors away. We had cameras installed at our last house, after all, that's how I was able to find out about Dale's affair with his colleague.

'It was a one-off, I swear to you.'

'You're a liar,' I screamed.

'It only happened because I'd had too much to drink.'

'You must think I'm totally stupid. She's been coming and going from here for weeks.'

'Where have you got that idea from? Of course she hasn't.'

'I found the footage you thought you'd deleted in the recycle bin.'

His face turned pale then.

If I hadn't spotted the missing time periods in the first place, I wouldn't have felt the need to dig deeper. Perhaps we'd have limped on a bit longer with me living in not-so-blissful ignorance.

We haven't got around to fixing cameras up here yet, at least Dale hasn't and possibly for the same reason. What if Rachel knows, better than I do, the inside of my bedroom?

This issue with my tyres is the last thing I need. I choke on a sob as I look back at the car. Could today get any worse before I've even got to work? I'm going to be late and I don't know what to do. I *needed* my car. It's bound to be that bloody man who's done this to me – who else would want to slash my tyres? What's to be gained by doing *this*? Unless it's some kind of threat. What else is he planning to slash? My neck?

If only we'd got around to installing the cameras. I'd have sorted them myself but, in my condition, I can't exactly be climbing up ladders. At least with cameras, I'd have *something* I could give the police for them to start taking my complaints about this man seriously.

I'd also have something to show Dale. He seems to think the whole stalking thing is nothing more than a figment of my imagination. For a moment, it crosses my mind to call him, to tell him what's happened and ask for his help, but that flies in the face of me disappearing for a few days. No, I've written the note and I've made up my mind. I'm leaving.

I check the registration of the Uber taxi against the one given on the app. I'm not taking any chances with my safety today. I can't cope with living at this high level of anxiety. I can't eat, I can't sleep and it feels like my stomach's bubbling with molten rock. While I'm away this weekend, I'm going to try to relax, then I'll get myself checked over by the midwife when I get back next week.

As I stand from my garden wall and climb into the back seat of the car, I'm still sensing someone's eyes on me. I look around but can't see anyone. If it's *him*, he must be hiding.

There are so many yet-to-be-had adventures for us, so many places we can visit, so many experiences we've yet to try together.

10

'IT'S NOT like you to be here *after* me.' Jae, the youngest of my two beauticians looks up from where she's making tea behind the counter and smiles. 'Do you want one?' She waves a mug in the air.

'She'll have been too busy getting spoiled for Valentine's Day,' Sian laughs.

If only.

'Are you doing anything special this evening,' Sian continues as she folds towels. 'Valentine's is falling on a good night, isn't it? Friday, I mean.' She continues waffling about a new restaurant her boyfriend has managed to get a table at and how she might be a bit worse for wear tomorrow morning. I hang my coat on the hook and head over to the counter. I can't let what's happened to my tyres stop me from going away. I can just book another Uber.

'*How* has Dale spoiled you then?' Jae asks, seemingly trying to keep the envy from her voice more than I'll be able to. She's recently been royally dumped by her boyfriend who reckoned she was getting too serious, too quickly. All because she mentioned her desire to eventually buy a house. *Men...*

'We'll probably exchange gifts this evening.' I force a smile. 'Anyway, I might not be in at all tomorrow, girls.' I look up from the appointment book. I'm going to have a ring round to see what jiggling about I can do for tomorrow's appointments and get some of them moved into next week. 'I'm feeling pretty exhausted and could use a break.'

'I can do a couple of extra hours.' Jae looks up from her tea-making.

'Oooh I said you'd be getting spoiled, didn't I?' Sian nudges me as she squeezes around the counter to put her phone in the drawer. 'So what's the lovely Dale planning?'

'I don't know yet,' I reply. I'm longing to tell them of my predicament but it wouldn't be very professional to bring my troubles into work. As far as they know, I'm a happily married woman with a rosy life and everything to look forward to. And it's down to me to make that my reality.

'You don't seem very excited about it – if you don't mind me saying.' Jae peers more closely at me. 'Are you sure you're OK, Tamara?'

The warmth and sympathy in her face and voice invite my old friends, the hot tears to stab at the backs of my eyes. Now I've passed the milestone of my twelve-week scan, this should be the happiest time of my life but it couldn't be any further away than that. I'm sick of feeling this crappy and can only pray that my little getaway plan doesn't backfire.

'Of course she is.' Sian glances at the clock and then across the courtyard. 'Why wouldn't she be? Oh look, my nine-thirty's on her way in. Nails, I think?'

'There's lots of nails booked in today,' says Jae. 'It's a good job we ordered all that Valentine red Shellac in.'

'You're right – it's looking like manicures for most of the morning.' I run my thumb down the list. 'Then it's Sian's turn to take an early lunch while me and Jae are both on facials.'

'I'm going out today for lunch,' Sian announces, a smug smile spreading across her face.

'He's taking you out for lunch *as well as* dinner?' Jae raises a perfectly arched eyebrow. 'Has he got a younger brother?'

Sian's smile broadens. 'I know.' She rests her palms on her chest and sways from side to side. 'I'm so lucky.'

I can't listen to any more. 'Right.' I hit the button on our piped music CD which loops all day. Our customers comment on how relaxed it helps them to feel but I barely notice it anymore. 'Let's get this party started.'

'It's all ready for you.' I smile at Becky, my first customer who's barely sat herself down in the waiting area. She's picked up a magazine but I haven't even given her a chance to start flicking through it. I need to get busy and I need to *keep* busy.

'Oooh, I can't decide between romantic pink or full-on sexy scarlet.' Becky runs her eyes among the rows of Shellac polish. 'I know – I'm like a kid in a cake shop.' She continues running her fingers over the assortment of coloured bottles until I feel like I'm going to implode.

Instead, I force a laugh. 'The red's very popular,' I tell her. 'And look, it contains a sparkle.'

'That's the one,' she cries, as though she's made the most important decision in the world. 'I'm being taken for a hot date tonight so all attention to detail is vital.'

'I thought you were married.' I sit facing her as I smooth a towel out between us and set up the nail dryer.

'I am.' She laughs. 'But I guess we're the lucky ones. My other half just gets more and more romantic as the years pass by. You've been married for a while too, haven't you? Are you getting spoiled today?'

'Fourteen years.' I can answer her first question easily

enough but not her second. I busy myself with getting everything else I'll need for the manicure ready so I can avoid Becky noticing I'm upset by her question. I wouldn't want her to see the tears glistening in my eyes.

'People do less time for murder,' laughs Jae's first customer as she takes a seat in the waiting area next to my table.

But as I glance from the window, I don't laugh back. Not after who I've just spotted.

'What's the matter?' As Jae comes out of the door of the room she'll be using, she and both our customers follow my gaze to where I'm staring out of the window.

There's no one else in the world I'd rather have by my side.

11

'You've gone as white as *this*, Tamara.' Jae waves the bottle of white polish we use for the tips in French manicures.

'It's just – no, you'll think I'm stupid.' I can't tear my eyes from the industrial bin where I'm certain I've just seen the man. The view from the window might be obscured by the floral hearts display, and he might have been a good distance away, but I'm sure it was him. As they always are when I encounter him, the hairs on the back of my neck are on end.

'How do you mean?'

'Someone's stalking me,' I reply, my eyes fixed on the window. He's disappeared. Typical. He always does when I want someone else to see him. Sometimes I wonder if perhaps I *am* going mad. Whether my hormones are causing me to see things no one else can. Gosh, I'm doing exactly what I vowed never to do – I've brought my shit into work.

'Stalking you.' Jae's voice rises. 'Really?'

I nod. 'It's this constant sense of being watched,' I reply, grateful to be able to spill it all, despite my previous vow. I just can't continue to carry all this on my own. Neither Dale nor Ali will take me seriously but Jae and Sian are different. After all, I pay their wages. 'He's been hanging around outside my house, and this morning, the tyres on my car have been slashed – all four of them.' I try to swallow the lump in my throat so I can turn my attention to what I'm supposed to be doing. 'Would you like them filing round or square?' I point at Becky's nails. 'I'm sorry. I promise I'll get myself together.' I nod towards a worried-looking Jae. 'Just pull the blinds down, please. It's the only way I'm going to get any work done today.'

'Do you need to take a break?' She asks.

'I'll be OK. I just need to keep busy. I'm sorry.'

'You don't have to apologise,' Becky says. 'Giving me a manicure seems pretty trivial in the face of what you've just said. Have you been to the police?'

'They weren't interested.' Anger prickles at the nape of my neck. 'I've been reading up on it and it seems the law encourages stalkers to attack and threaten.'

'*Encourages?*' Jae's customer's voice almost squeaks as she gets to her feet. 'How can that be?'

'The stalker gets away with making someone's life hell. The police will only act when they do something to cause their victim harm. I've read up on it.'

'But your tyres,' Jae replies, making no move to take her client to the treatment room even though she's got to her feet. She seems more bothered about me which is a comfort. It certainly makes a change. 'Surely now—'

'I've no proof it was *him* who cut my tyres,' I say. 'No one other than me has even seen him outside my house. Of course, I'm going to report it, but for now, I'm just glad to be keeping occupied at work. So I guess we'd all better crack on.'

Jae beckons her customer into the treatment room while I begin pushing Becky's cuticles back. 'So enough of all that anyway. Where did you say your hubby was taking you tonight?'

Becky's frown becomes a smile as she waxes lyrical about

where she's going and what she's planning to wear, while my mind wanders off as I paint her nails. I wonder how Dale will react when he finds my note. Will he try calling or will he just leave me alone? Will I even reply if he *does* call or will I leave him to stew? Where am I even going to go tonight? Lunchtime can't come quickly enough so I can decide my course of action. My head feels jumbled and I just want to straighten out my thinking. But I feel safer here in the salon that's my cocoon, with my lovely girls and customers for company.

'He said I need to make sure I'm home at three pm as something's being delivered.' Becky scrunches her face in excitement to which I make myself crack a smile. My face will probably ache by lunchtime.

It's the same all morning. Customer after customer boasts about the flowers or chocolates they've received, their plans for the forthcoming evening and what outfit they plan to wear. If I *was* returning home, it would be the same old, same old sort of evening. For me, there'd be no flowers, chocolates or fancy meals. There are also plenty of male customers in the shop throughout the morning. All buy gift vouchers to give to their partners as a Valentine's gift. Some might bemoan this 'lack of imagination,' but at least they've bought a gift with some thought. I'd love *any* sort of gesture from Dale.

He said he'd be working late so who knows how long I'd be waiting at home on my own if I *did* go home. I'd only be fretting about who might be watching my house and waiting to slash more than my tyres. I'd also be watching for Dale's arrival, and to see whether he gets immediately collared by Rachel as he parks his car. I still can't shake the thought that Dale might have sent the roses and the card that are sitting so proudly on her windowsill.

It's a relief to close the door on the upstairs treatment room and get on with my twelve o'clock facial in my favourite room in the salon. I always light it with candles. At least, other than the preliminaries, I don't have to make mindless conversation with my customer about Valentine's Day.

'Would you like relaxing or uplifting oils,' I ask her. She takes almost as long deliberating over her decision as Becky did with her nail colour, and something that's normally against my grain when I'm at work snakes over me – irritation.

My thoughts wander as I cleanse and tone her skin. Am I doing the right thing? Should I *really be* running away this evening? After all, I could change my mind and still go home, unpack my holdall and tear up that note before Dale arrives home and reads it. I could try my hardest to make things special for when he returns. Maybe get dressed up, cook him a nice meal and try to act like we used to. He'd be none the wiser.

But there's no denying that whichever way I jump, my marriage is completely on the line. And if I do what I've always done, I'll continue to receive what I've always received.

Lies, indifference, loneliness and misery.

~

Tonight, I won't have to wait any longer.

12

'Oooh look.' Sian points at what looks like a white card propped up by the kettle. 'This came through the door while I was out at lunch.' She shrugs out of her oversized coat, shakes out her long blonde hair and heads towards the embossed envelope. 'I found it on the mat.'

'I never heard the doorbell. Did you?' I glance at Jae who shakes her head, her brunette bun wobbling with the movement. 'Is that my name on the front?'

'It sure is.' Sian passes me the card. 'I saw Dale when I was heading onto the main street earlier.'

'Really? Was he on his way here?'

'I guess he must have been.' Her face darkens. 'I don't know what was wrong with him though.'

'What do you mean?' Oh God, what if he's found my note already.

'Well, I asked what he was planning for your Valentine's evening and he told me to mind my own business.' Her voice rises.

'I'm sure he was joking,' says Jae.

'Maybe.' Then she brightens again. 'Anyway, it's good to see a smile back on your face again, Tamara. You've seemed a bit distracted today.'

She wasn't down here when we were discussing the stalker and my tyres but no doubt, Jae will fill her in.

'Is it a Valentine's card?' Jae sniffs and raises her eyes to the ceiling. 'Am I the only one out of the three of us who hasn't got a card?'

'It's just a note.' I laugh. 'It won't be the first time Dale's got his PA to do his organising for him, or his letter writing, judging by this writing.' I study the calligraphy both on the envelope and on the note itself.

'So hopefully you can also expect a bouquet of roses to be delivered during the afternoon as well. What does it say then?' They both crane their necks. 'Or are we being too nosy?'

I've planned us a Valentine's evening. Come as you are, just bring yourself. Poppy Cottage, Settle Road, Wrigglesworth. Can't wait to see you.

'Ooh, how romantic.' A customer who's waiting to pay leans in to look.

'*And* up in the Yorkshire Dales,' Sian adds. 'It sounds like your other half's pulling out all the stops. Anyway,' – She glances at the door, – 'it looks like my one o'clock's here.'

'Are you going out for lunch today, Tamara?' Jae threads her arms into her coat. 'Or do you want me to grab you a sandwich while I'm out?' She gives me a knowing look. She probably knows as well as I do that staying safely inside here is my preferred option.

'Grab us both one.' I open the cash box and slide a note from it. They're great, my two girls and we all look after each other. My only gripe is because I've trained them both along-side their college courses and they're fresh out of school, they make me feel really old, especially Jae, so young and petite. 'And buy Sian a cake for her afternoon tea so she doesn't feel left out. She'll have already eaten with her boyfriend, won't she?'

'It's lovely to see that you've perked up,' Jae says as she opens the door. 'Two out of three of us isn't bad, I suppose. You must be really happy to have your cottage to look forward to later.'

'Thanks,' I reply. 'And don't worry – your time will come. You'll be snapped up soon enough. In the meantime, you should enjoy being young and free.'

She gives me a look which conveys, *that's easy for you to say* as she closes the door after herself.

I *am* happy. A little shocked but definitely happy. Perhaps this is why Dale left so early this morning – clearly, he had a surprise to get ready for me.

Receiving that note has brought my hunger back a little. Since the positive test just before Christmas, a combination of anxiety and pregnancy sickness has robbed me of my appetite and I must be one of the few expectant mothers who've lost half a stone rather than gaining it in these early months.

Even though I'm brighter than I was, I still don't feel like leaving the salon. Not after what's happened to my tyres and not after sensing someone near those bins earlier this morning. Even if I *am* beginning to doubt my judgement, I'll stay in my sanctuary with its soothing music and the intermingled scents of nail polish and essential oils.

This might be my workplace but it's my happy place. And Dale's always said how proud he is of me for building it up from scratch by myself. As he's boasted to our friends when we've been out, no one's ever given me anything. The only thing my parents gave me was heartache, guilt and the need to endure fortnightly prison visits for nearly eight years.

'See you on Tuesday,' Sian says as I slide my holdall from under the counter. Her smile turns into a puzzled expression. 'I thought you didn't know until lunchtime about your cottage jaunt.' She points at my bag.

'Gym stuff,' I reply. 'I was planning to do a gentle yoga class.' No one needs to know I was planning to disappear for a couple of days. Instead, I'll have the chance to talk with Dale later and I feel sure that now he's made this effort for our marriage, we'll be able to sort everything out. 'Anyway,' I nod from her to Jae. 'Thanks so much for helping me cover tomorrow's appointments. There'll be something extra in your pay packets this month to say thank you.'

'Have a fantastic weekend,' they chorus. I open the door and check left to right first and then across the courtyard.

'Are you looking for *him* from this morning?' asks Jae.

'Who?' I glance back to notice Sian's inquisitive face.

'Just someone who's been hanging around,' I reply.

'Do you want me to walk you to the taxi?'

I smile at Jae. 'That's really nice of you. But no, just keep an eye on me until I'm safely inside and then make sure you lock this door until you're ready to leave.

The door falls closed behind me. and I dash across the courtyard to the waiting Uber.

Despite my constant state of high alert because of the stalker, a frisson of excitement dances in my belly as I slide into the back seat and tell the driver where I'm going. For the first time in a while, I have a really strong feeling that everything's going to turn out just fine.

There's not much I don't know about you.
And I can't wait for you to discover
everything about me.

13

'ARE you sure we're going to the right place?' I lean forward in the seat. We haven't passed another house for well over a mile. Surely there must be *some* civilisation around wherever Dale's picked for us to stay overnight. I'm all for seclusion but this is in another league.

'That's what it's saying on my sat nav.' The taxi driver points at it. 'Are you sure you've given me the right address?'

'I'll double-check my note.' I tug it from the pocket in my tunic for what feels like the millionth time since it was posted through the salon door. 'Yeah, it's the right one. Poppy Cottage, Settle Road. So just keep driving.'

'It looks like this so-called cottage is in the arse end of nowhere,' the driver laughs. 'I hope your other half has brought in plenty of supplies.'

'I'm sure he will have done.' I smile to myself, still unable to believe that Dale's gone to all this trouble. Most of the time, he doesn't have a romantic bone in his body. I'll never forget when he proposed. We laugh about it now but I can't imagine anyone's ever received a less romantic proposal. It's not as if he even planned it and if it wasn't for his mother's jokey comments when we went for dinner at her house, he'd probably never have given it a second thought. All our friends were getting married, but I got the impression that the prospect had never even crossed his mind.

'Should I be buying myself a hat yet?' His mum had asked, laughing. 'You two *have* been together since you were teenagers and *everyone* keeps asking me.'

'Kathryn!' His father had nudged her.

'Besides...' She was undeterred. 'We want to be granny and grandpa while we've still got plenty of energy.'

'I suppose you could get yourself one,' Dale replied as he shovelled more mash onto his fork. Meanwhile, his dad looked like he might choke on the sprout he had just popped into his mouth.

'What?' I'd shot him a look. 'What do you mean?'

'Mum *could* buy herself a hat if she really wants to.' He grinned as if it wasn't a bad idea. As if he'd thought of it himself.

'Oooh. I think we need a glass of something sparkly to celebrate.' She rushed to the fridge.

I rested my fork down. 'Is this your idea of a marriage proposal, Dale?'

'Well you *do* want to get married, don't you?' He stabbed at a Yorkshire pudding. 'You've banged on about it often enough.'

'Well, yes, but not like this, I mean, aren't you supposed to get down on one knee or something?'

His mum had laughed her head off at her son's lack of romance but nonetheless, was clearly delighted. 'Oh, he's as bad as his dad. He was just the same when we were planning to get married. In fact, it was *me* who ended up asking *him*, wasn't it, Tom?'

So that was that. I chose my own engagement ring, which Dale just footed the bill for. As an IT Consultant, he's not exactly short of money. We had a meal to celebrate but it was me who had to order the champagne.

We haven't passed another house or car for miles. I hope we haven't gone off course – I can't wait to see my husband now, especially since we didn't speak this morning and were barely speaking last night. I'm over the moon that everything's going to be alright. It would have been a miserable few days if I'd been forced to follow through with this morning's plan.

'This looks like it could be it.' The wheels of the Uber crunch up beside a picturesque cottage, lit up with lamplight at every window and with ivy climbing around the door. Excitement bubbles in my belly. It's perfect and I'm so happy that Dale's gone to all this trouble. It's little wonder there was no card this morning. Not when he was planning all this.

'Enjoy your evening,' the driver calls after me. 'And hopefully, when I clock off, I won't be able to open my front door for the deluge of Valentine's cards that will be blocking the hallway.'

'Fingers crossed,' I call back as he begins to turn his car in the narrow lane.

I pause at the gate and look down at my leggings and tunic. I should have got ready *before* getting here. Dale's finally made this effort for our marriage and I should have done too. I could have had a shower and done my makeup at the salon if I'd have been more organised. Oh well, I'm here now and once I've thanked him for doing all this, I'll get sorted.

I push the gate open and head up the gravel path to the door. I can't wait to see if it's as lovely inside as it looks from out here. The rumble of the taxi's engine fades into the night, leaving me in a silence only broken by an occasional hoot of an owl. I look all around me, but in the darkness, can hardly see a thing. Anyone could be lying in wait for me and no one would ever know.

Perhaps I should have asked the driver to wait until I knew I had the right place before disappearing, *and* until I was safely inside. He's right, this really is the arse end of nowhere. I push the ivy which conceals the sign. *Poppy Cottage.* No, this is it.

Just as I'm about to ring the bell, I spot a card taped below it with the same style of writing as the note that arrived at the salon. Oooh, it's looking like Dale has set up some kind of trail for me. Wait until I tell my sister about this – she won't believe me.

Come inside and follow the petals. I'll see you shortly.

∽

Each moment has led towards the one that's coming our way.

14

How mysterious. And how unlike Dale! All I can think is that he must have got this idea from all the reels he watches on social media. I'm certainly not complaining though.

I push the door open, and am immediately hit by the heat of the cottage and the wonderful smell of... I think it's my favourite – pepper sauce. Oh my word, he's even cooking us a meal. He hasn't done this since he was trying to impress me right at the beginning of our relationship. He's even playing my favourite music, Ed Sheeran. I bought us tickets for his concert last year.

Everywhere I look, there are petals. He must have spent a fortune, given that it's Valentine's Day, when all florists triple the price of red roses. I have to stifle a gasp as I look down at the doormat and then begin following the trail across the hallway. After all my moaning and being upset, I can't believe what he's done for me. Well, for us. My sister was right, things *did* need to change. And now, finally, it looks like they are. Perhaps I *haven't* married someone just like my father after all and I'm *not* on course to lead the same life of misery as my mother. Dale and I have put the past behind us and when the baby comes, the three of us are going to be the happiest of families.

It doesn't feel right to enter the house and head straight upstairs without at least announcing my arrival. I call out, 'Dale, it's me, I'm here. I'll just freshen up, then I'll be right with you.'

There's a clattering of pans from the room at the end of the hallway and a bang of what sounds like an oven door. My husband always gets flustered when he's immersed in something, particularly when it's outside his comfort zone, like cooking. He's a whizz at computers but with anything practical, he really struggles. I should probably leave him to it and, like he wants me to, get on with following this trail.

There's another note taped to the bottom of the handrail of the stairs.

Go up, I've run a bath for you. Enjoy!

I smile. It's a shame he won't be sitting in it already, waiting. I can't remember the last time the two of us took a bath. I really hope he's booked this place for at least two nights. We'll be able to make up for so much lost time.

I kick off my pumps and head up the stairs, my feet sinking into the thick pile of the carpet as I'm greeted by the scent of ylang-ylang. Wow! He's filled me a bath alright. More rose petals float on its surface and he must have lit around twenty candles. There's a glass of bubbly waiting on the side of the bath and a fluffy white robe draped over the towel rail.

I pick the glass up by the stalk. He's said before that I should be OK with just one glass while I'm expecting, but as I've already told him, this baby is too precious for us to take any chances. I sniff at it. Perhaps it's alcohol free but I'm not taking the risk. It fizzes as I pour it into the sink before refilling the glass with water. He's not to know I haven't drunk it.

Tears stab at my eyes as I let my hair out of its ponytail. I must mean more to my husband than he's ever let on. I'm blown away by what he's done for me. I wonder if he went back home this morning. If perhaps he saw my note – maybe that's what's ignited this behaviour? He's certainly never done anything like it before.

'Are you sure you won't come up here and join me in the bath?' I call from the landing. He doesn't respond but there's more clattering about from the kitchen. Even if he heard me, the chances are that he's juggling more than one course for our dinner so he's probably up to his neck. Hopefully, he's poured himself a glass of something as well, so that he's not too stressed when we finally sit down together to eat.

It's only when I begin to peel off my clothes that a cold feeling creeps up my spine. Could I be kidding myself? Dale knows I'm not drinking so the glass of bubbly could mean all this isn't really meant for me? What if there's been some kind of mistake? His secretary could have delivered his note *for* him and assumed it was for me when really it wasn't. Perhaps this is all meant for Rachel. Or even someone else.

But I'm here now, so I do everything I can to shake the thought away as I lower myself into the bath. I'm being ridiculous and should just really enjoy my husband's wonderful surprise. And it's a gorgeous bathroom. Quaint and cosy. I really could live somewhere like this. Our house is great but hasn't got the character of this little cottage with its beams, tiny windows and low ceilings. Me and my husband, cosily tucked away from the rest of the world.

I'm surprised Dale hasn't at least come up to say hello. Still, this is probably all part of this evening's treat – he's giving me some time to unwind after work and then we'll have a lovely night.

But as I sip at my water, I can't relax. It feels too self-indulgent when I know he'll be wrestling with timings and getting everything perfect in the kitchen. I should go and help. Besides, I want to let him know just how grateful I am, and how I can't wait to see what he's got in store for the rest of the evening.

I'm also anxious to find out whether he read my note. If he didn't, then I'll keep it a secret. Instead, I'll ensure I'm the first one back into the house when we return home, and I'll grab it before he sees it. Things are on the up between us and I'm not going to be the one who ruins it.

Wrapping myself in the fluffy robe, I climb out of the bath, eager to investigate the rest of the upstairs of this beautiful cottage. However, there's only one other room up here – the bedroom. I poke my head around the door and have to stop myself from gasping.

You'll look beautiful in this.

He's laid a gorgeous deep red dress and some lacy black underwear out on the bed. I head over to it and one by one, I pick up the garments. He must have checked in my wardrobe and drawers at home as everything's exactly the correct size. There's a shoe box on the floor. Size six kitten heels. It reminds me of when he said something rare and romantic when we first got together, *I like you in heels as I don't have to stoop as far to kiss you.*

I smile at the memory as I look into the full-length mirror, running my hands down my midriff. My belly is still flat though not as sculpted as it was. I can't wait to see the first swell of the baby and even more excitingly, when it begins to kick. I have visions of Dale with his hand resting here at every opportunity as we eagerly wait for our turn to become a proper family at last.

The bedroom is dimly lit by lamps, all furnished in pine and with immaculate white bedding, carpet and curtains. It would be *lovely* to make a weekend of it here. It was pitch black when the taxi dropped me off but I'll bet nearby, there are some romantic walks. There's a second note beneath the first one.

And you'll look even more beautiful out of it.

Thank goodness. He's barely seemed attracted to me since I became pregnant but this note suggests otherwise. I just want to get down there and give him a big kiss. I smile as I quickly dress, clipping my bra and taking time with my stockings. I don't want to ladder them after he's gone to all the trouble of picking them out, no doubt from some swanky lingerie shop. Then I smooth the dress over my body. It fits like a second skin.

What he hasn't thought about though is my hair or makeup. However, he'll know from the umpteen times I've told him to find something in my bag that I've always got a hairbrush and some face powder in the back pocket. Luckily I've got my full makeup kit in my holdall though I apply it sparingly. He's often told me that he prefers my face bare of make-up and my hair natural rather than pinned up or straightened. Like Rachel over the road. But then she doesn't need makeup like I do.

Bloody hell, why on earth am I thinking about her again? What Dale's done here tonight is way beyond anything I could have dreamed of, and the last thing I want to do is sour my mood before I go down to see him. Or, more importantly, *his* mood. There's another note pinned just above the door handle.

I can't wait to have dinner with you. Don't be long.

I can't wait either. I scrunch my hair between my fists until it curls around my shoulders and slide some lipstick over my lips.

With my new kitten heels sinking into the carpet, I head

downstairs feeling great in all the clothes my lovely husband has picked out. It's the first time in ages I've felt this confident about my appearance. And I always feel better when I'm wearing matching underwear – something I haven't made any effort with since the positive pregnancy test. All that's mattered to me is the baby. The music has been silenced – I'll have to ask him to turn it back on. As I reach the bottom step, a swarm of butterflies has taken up residence in my abdomen. I pray it *is* me he's expecting and that he's not disappointed with what he sees when I stand in front of him. Hopefully, I'll see the same look in his eyes that used to melt me when we first got together.

'Dale.' I tap at the door as I push it open. 'Are you ready for me?'

He's got his back to me as I step into the kitchen and I'm taken aback that he's wearing shorts and a t-shirt at this time of year. And he's barefoot which shows how relaxed he must be here. This is going to be such a great night. My breath catches with the slap of heat and the aroma of something sweet.

'I can't believe what you've done for me.' I allow the door to fall closed. 'This is absolutely amazing – thank you so much!'

I gasp yet again as he turns around to face me, and my body freezes in terror.

For the person who ran me a bath, poured me a drink and is cooking my dinner is *not* my husband.

～

Our time has come.
And I can't wait to spend it together.

15

I TWIST on my heel back towards the door. But the man lurches forward and we reach it at the same time.

'Please, there's been some mistake. I've obviously got the wrong message.' I'm struggling to get any breath in.

'There's no mistake, Tamara.' His voice is gentle. Menacingly gentle. And he knows my name.

'Who are you?' My voice shakes. 'My husband is supposed to be here – he sent—' I need to calm down. I need to breathe. I need to get out of this house.

'I thought you wanted this too.'

'Wanted what? Who the hell are you anyway?' Oh my God. I could really be in trouble here.

'Look, I know it's a shock, but I promise this evening will be everything you've been waiting for.'

'Please, just let me go.' I step to the side. Surely he's not going to stop me.

He also takes a step to the side, once again blocking my path to the door. 'You look absolutely beautiful, Tamara.' He runs his eyes down my body. His gaze makes the hairs on the back of my neck stand on end. 'Just like I knew you would. Does everything fit you OK?'

My handbag, holdall, purse and phone are all up in the bedroom. *If only I'd brought everything back downstairs.* But that's only *stuff*. Nothing's as important as getting away from him.

'I erm, I need to get something from the bedroom.'

'Wait – just let me pour you some more champagne.' He steers me towards the table and I move like a clockwork doll. Flight has clearly turned to fright and I freeze beneath his hands.

I stand in front of the table, my body rigid with fear. As he opens the fridge and I glimpse his side profile, I'm almost certain it's the man who's been stalking me. I've never seen him close up, but it *has* to be him. He's the same height and build, has the same spike of hair – everything. And it's the wearing of the shorts too. Maybe, if he's fantasised about getting me here like this for some time, he'll just want to spend time with me and won't be harbouring any plans to cause me harm. Perhaps it's just his sick infatuation at play and if I go along with his game for long enough to throw him off guard, there'll be a window of opportunity for me to bolt back out into that lane under the cover of darkness, with or without my things from upstairs.

'Have a seat.' He carries the champagne bottle to the table and pulls one of the chairs out, smiling a smile that makes me even more terrified. I'm shaking from the outside in as I lower myself to the seat. The table wouldn't be out of place in a swanky restaurant – laden with glasses, cutlery, candles – all set for a meal for two. He begins to pour.

While he's got his hands full, now's my chance to make another run for it. I jump from my seat, dart across the kitchen and tug at the door I've just entered by, dashing through it and grabbing my pumps from where I kicked them off on the doormat when I first arrived. I'll swap these stupid heels for them when I get back onto the lane. I yank my coat from where I draped it over the bannister and lurch to the front door.

Which he's locked when I was upstairs.

While I tug at the handle as though that could magically make the door suddenly open, he comes up behind me, his shadow looming larger over mine against the door. 'I thought you'd be happy.' His breath is on my neck as he gently removes my pumps from my hand and discards them. 'I've been so looking forward—'

'You can't keep me here like this.' I spin around to face him, holding my coat as a barrier between us. In any other circumstances, he'd be a good-looking man but in this particular situation, he's terrifying. 'My husband will come looking for me and...' My voice trails off as I realise the predicament I've found myself in.

Dale *won't* be looking for me. It's getting towards eight o'clock. Instead, any time at all, he'll arrive home to find my note. If he hasn't already. Then he'll no doubt hit the whiskey or seek out some alternative company for the evening.

'I thought you felt the same way as me.' He looks almost hurt.

'Whatever gave you that idea?' This isn't happening. It really can't be happening.

'It's just – oh, it doesn't matter.' He pulls at my coat and I tug it back. 'Look, you're here now. *We're* here. Let's just enjoy our meal and get to know each other better, shall we?'

'Over my dead body.' I push past him and manage to get to the bottom of the stairs before he takes hold of me from behind. The way he's gripping my shoulders says he's reminding me who the strongest person is here. What a stupid thing to say. *Over my dead body.* Talk about tempting fate.

'Don't be like this, Tamara.' His voice is full of anguish as he lets me go. 'Please don't be like this.'

Oh my God. He's an absolute nutter. I need to get to my

phone. Somehow I need to call for help. I'll pretend I'm going to be sick so I can get to the bathroom. The way I'm feeling, I may not have to pretend for much longer.

'I don't feel too good.' I lean against the bannister. 'I think I'm going to be—' I clasp a hand across my mouth, turn again and dart up the stairs but he's hot on my heels and steers me into the bathroom as soon as I get to the top.

'I'll be right outside, Tamara,' he says. 'I won't leave you alone when you're not well. Not like *he* would.'

He must mean Dale and is evidently nursing hatred towards him being that *he's* the one I've chosen to spend my life with. I slam the door in his face and my fingers reach to slide the bolt across. But there isn't one. Shit. In one move, I'm at the window, wrestling with the catch. Let's see if I can re-enact the skills I possessed in my teens of shimmying down a drainpipe. But back then I'd be wearing trainers and jeans. And I wouldn't be three months pregnant.

The window's locked — of course it is. I beat at the sill with my fists, I have to get out of here, by any means possible. But being a cottage, the frosted panes between the mullions are tiny – not big enough for a small child to fit through, let alone a five-foot-eight woman, even if I do succeed in smashing the glass. But I can still raise the alarm and yell outside for help just in case there are any other cottages further up this lane. My sobs become more desperate as my eyes dart around the room, fruit-lessly searching for something, *anything*, to help me get out of here. I yelp as the door swings open and he stoops beneath the frame. He doesn't speak, he just stands there, staring at me. The fight seeps from me as our eyes lock in stalemate.

I stand in the centre of the bathroom, fighting to get my breath. 'Please just let me go home.'

'You look exactly like my wife did,' he says, seeming to ignore the fact that I was clearly searching for another way to escape. '*Exactly* like she did. Right down to the slant of your eyes and the way your hair waves. You even talk the same.'

'What do you mean, *did*?' A chill snakes up my spine as my knees buckle and I lower myself to the edge of the bath. The bubble-covered petals are still popping inside it. Really, I know exactly what he means.

'She died. Six years ago.' The intensity of his gaze doesn't waver. He's got the most piercing blue eyes I've ever seen and chunky arms that look like they should make you feel safe. However, I've never felt more unsafe in my entire life. This is an absolute nightmare.

'Wh-what did she die of?' I grip the rim of the bath.

'I really don't want to talk about that. Not tonight. I only want to talk about *you*.' He still isn't taking his eyes off me.

'I just need to go. There's been some—'

'Seriously, you don't know how wonderful it is that you're here, Tamara.' His face breaks into a dimpled smile, white teeth and everything. 'I've been dreaming of this moment for months.'

'But I'm married.'

'On paper maybe. Listen to me, sweetheart. Everything's going to be different now – for both of us. I'm going to make you so happy.'

'But I don't know you – I don't even know your name.'

'It's Martin.' His smile broadens. 'Look, I'm aware that this must all feel strange. But after tonight, when you know me as well as I know you—'

'Just because you've been watching me doesn't mean you *know* me.' I hoist the dress up on my chest. The last thing I want is this weirdo gawping at my cleavage.

'Surely all *this*,' he waves his arms around. 'Proves how *much* I love you. I only want the best for you.'

'How can you *love* me – this is the first time we've even

spoken to each other,' I reply. 'And I just want to go home – that's the *best* thing for me.' It's on the tip of my tongue to mention the baby. But I'm worried that may put me even more at risk. No, I'm better to keep quiet about that for now.

'This could be your home. I know the owner of this place – I could rent it for us. And I know how much you love the Yorkshire Dales. There's *nothing* I haven't discovered about you over the last few years.'

'Like what?' His words creep over me like a rash.

'Oh, your favourite music, as I've already proven.' He leans into the doorframe. 'I know what you like to read, what winds you up, I know you're scared of the dark.'

'Only when *you're* outside my house, watching me. Do you know how petrified I've been, knowing someone's out there all the time?'

'I just love you – why can't you accept that? I've loved you from the first moment I set eyes on you.'

'Only because I remind you of your wife. But I'm not her, Martin. I'm Tamara. I'm *Dale's* wife.' While I keep him talking, I'm scanning the room, a section at a time, looking for something I can weaponise. There isn't so much as a vase in here that I could swing at him. It's as if he's moved everything out of my way.

'*He* doesn't love you. Anyone can see that. Things will be so different for both of us from now on.' He straightens himself up. 'You've just got to trust me.'

'Trust you.' It's my turn to laugh. 'You've been scaring me out of my wits for years.'

'I'm sorry for that – truly I am.' He steps forward and stretches his arm out. I shrink back from him. 'I never wanted to scare you. I just wanted to be a part of your life. You're my second chance – my chance to put everything right.'

'You'll *never* be part of my life.' Seeing another opportunity now that he's stepped away from the door, I jump up from the edge of the bath and barge past him. This is my chance to get to my phone. And maybe I can attract attention from the upstairs window at the front of the cottage.

16

'YOU WON'T FIND a way out of that window.' His voice, suddenly colder than it's been so far, is right behind me as I tug at the bedroom curtains. 'Or through *any* of the windows. And even if you could.' He spins me around to face him. 'Why would you want to leave me now?'

Something sags inside me. I can't get out of here so I'm going to have to play along until I can escape. It's the only way to ensure I keep myself and the baby safe. I've got to hang onto the belief that his warped obsession means his plans for me aren't anything sinister. That he just wants to spend time with me. After all, I remind him of his dead wife. I'd try and claw his eyes out or get him by the balls if I wasn't pregnant but I've got to stay calm. It isn't just *me* that's at risk here.

'Suppose I stay and eat the meal with you, Martin? Then, can I go home?' As if I'm having to ask permission. I thought my life felt rough this morning, what with the situation with Dale and that woman from across the road, but that was a walk in the park compared to where I've ended up.

'Let's see how things go between us, shall we?' He beckons

towards the door. 'Come on.' I take a brief glance around the room as I follow him onto the landing. There's no sign of any of my belongings. He must have moved everything while I was in the bathroom. But he only had a minute or two, so not long enough to move it very far. I'll get another chance to get up here and have a proper look.

I could eat a little of the meal but then pretend that I only want to leave because I don't want to sleep under the same roof as him – not until I've got to know him better. I can somehow make him believe we're spending some sort of date night together, and that I'll see him *next* time. Then I'll scarper and call the police. I can pull this off, I'm sure I can.

'So what have you cooked?' I load as much enthusiasm as I can muster into my voice. I'll do whatever I have to do to get out of here safely.

He turns back at the top of the stairs which are still littered with rose petals, his face relaxing with happiness. 'Follow me and you'll find out.'

The cold hand of fear clutches at my chest and stops me dead in my tracks at the top of the stairs. What if he's laced my food with some drug or other so he can do whatever he wants with me? Oh my God, there's my baby to think of. No, if he was going to do that, he'd have done it *already,* surely. He thinks I drank a full glass of champagne when I believed it was Dale who'd poured it for me. He'd be asking questions if something was supposed to have taken effect by now and obviously hasn't.

If only it *was* Dale who'd poured that first drink. Tears prickle at my eyes as I follow Martin down the stairs. Dale will have found my note by now. But after the mood he was in last night and the abrupt way he left this morning, I can't imagine he'll even contemplate looking for me. But perhaps the girls at work will raise the alarm if Martin doesn't let me go and I don't turn in tomorrow.

'What's the matter now?' Martin turns on the bottom step as once more, I stop dead in my tracks.

Of course I won't be turning into work tomorrow. Sian and Jae think I'm away for a romantic weekend with my husband. So if I don't get out of this cottage tonight, *no one* is going to be looking for me unless my sister realises I'm missing.

'Nothing. Go on.' I want to say *let's get this over and done with* but I need to play along and lull him into a false sense of security. The police will have to do something about him *now*. Before, they were fobbing me off with, *we can't arrest someone for standing around on your street. He's got to actually do something which hurts or threatens to hurt you.*

How about luring someone under false pretences to an isolated cottage, locking them inside and hiding all their belongings? The smell of food and the slap of kitchen heat turns my stomach as I re-enter the kitchen but as he gestures to the table, I've no choice other than to take a seat at it.

'Everything's just about ready,' he says, his voice filled with pride. 'Hopefully, the peppercorn sauce won't have spoiled for being reheated. And our steaks will just be a few minutes.' There's a sizzle as he turns one over.

While he has his back to me, I glance around the kitchen, making mental notes on any locations he might have hidden the keys to the front door while I was in the bath. He'll have to go to the toilet at some point and surely he won't make me accompany him. I'll have the chance to search then.

There are several drawers, a ceramic jar on the windowsill and a couple of pots that are contenders for hiding places. They'll also be useful as something I could knock him out with. The keys could be anywhere though and like the rest of the house, the window panes in the kitchen are too small to be able to smash my way out of and escape from. The keys or finding my phone is my only hope. Or whacking him over the head. As well as the ceramic jar, there are the pans I could use but right now he's standing next to them. There are a row of drawers behind him, probably where the knives are kept. I hope it won't go that far as I'm scared of hurting the baby with any sudden physical exertion. I'm probably causing it enough damage with the stress I'm under. I take some deep breaths like I would in a yoga class – I must calm myself down.

'Are you OK, Tamara?'

As well as can be expected when being held in a house by a lunatic, I want to say, but instead, I just nod.

'It's well done, just how you like it. Without a hint of blood on your plate.' He smiles as he slides the plate in front of me, the smell of the food causing me to gulp bile. He's acting as though we've been married for ten years and he's just cooked me a special meal.

'How do you know?' He's right about how I like my steak cooked. He's also made me my favourite accompaniment to a steak. Peppercorn sauce, onion rings, a large mushroom, chunky chips, half a tomato, grilled one side only, and not just *any* peas, but petit pois. It's as though I've placed an order in a restaurant.

'I was once sitting at a table in an adjoining booth when you were having a meal with *him*.' His smile fades momentarily at the mention of Dale, but then brightens again. 'Anyway, you're with *me* now and that's the way it's going to stay from now on.'

I stare back at him. In the looks department, he's exactly the type I'd normally go for. Dark-haired, blue-eyed, broad, tall, and athletic but there's a wild look in his eyes which is congruent to the situation he's trapped me in.

I still can't believe I'm here. How could I have fallen for those notes? I should have known that Dale doesn't have it in him to plan such an elaborate surprise. It's also warped that this Martin seems to know more about me than my husband does.

'Oh, I nearly forgot.' He rises from his chair, dropping the napkin from his lap as he goes. He grabs a bottle of wine from the counter and returns to his seat. 'Chateauneuf Du Pape,' he announces as he turns two glasses over. 'I got it especially for you. It'll go perfectly with your steak.'

I watch as he fills my glass. 'Can I have some water, please?'

'But this is your favourite.' The hurt look has returned.

'Yes, but I always have water with a meal. You should know that.' I force a smile. 'Since you know everything else about me.'

He heads over to the fridge and fills another wine glass from the water dispenser. 'Ice?' It's as if he can't do enough for me. I shake my head.

'Taste your steak, Tamara. I want to know if I've cooked it right.'

He's locked me into this house, confiscated my phone and belongings and is effectively holding me against my will. Yet he's wanting to know if he's cooked my steak correctly. This is surreal.

I rest my hands on the cutlery and then in the pause of his expectation, I rise from the chair. 'I'll just see if there are a couple of steak knives, shall I? Make it easier to cut.'

He jumps up so fast after me, that he knocks his wine glass over, sending a red streak across the immaculate white table-cloth. 'There aren't any actually. I've already looked.' He points at my chair. 'So why don't you sit back down and tell me if I've got your steak right.'

'But I won't be able to cut into it.'

He waits until I drop back into my seat before reaching for a towel and dabbing at the spilt wine. 'It's a good job I bought a case of the stuff, isn't it?' He grins as he grabs the neck of the bottle. 'I'd better have a refill.'

This is what I need – for him to drink plenty. At least then, he may end up needing the loo sooner. The fact that he's serving us from the same bottle allays some of my fear that the wine could be laced. But I'm still unsure about the food. Not that I've any sort of appetite. He saws into his steak with his butter knife.

'It's a good job I got fillets, isn't it? Easy to slice through. You're a woman after my own heart – with expensive tastes. I can't believe how well-suited we are.'

I watch as he cuts into his steak, a dab of blood mixing into his peppercorn sauce. Then he pops it into his mouth and begins to chew. 'Perfect,' he proclaims. 'Now let's hear what you think. Come on, Tamara, it'll be getting cold.' He nods at my plate.

I don't know how I'm going to get any of this food down, but I've got to try if I'm going to keep up some kind of pretence. I stab at the steak with my fork and slice a morsel of the meat surprisingly easily with my butter knife. I turn it this way and that on my fork. There doesn't seem to be anything on it other than a scrape of peppercorn sauce. I have my favourite meal in front of me yet feel like I could vomit. How can I swallow food this man's prepared?

'Eat,' he insists. 'You look like you could do with a good meal inside you.'

I shove the piece of steak into my mouth. He watches me intently as I chew and finally manage to swallow.

'Good?'

I nod. What else can I do? Then I reach for my water. Even if I wasn't pregnant I wouldn't be touching any of that wine. I'm going to need my wits about me to escape. But I have a part to play. I'll try and get a few of these peas down and look like I'm enjoying the meal he's cooked.

'He doesn't deserve you, you know?'

'Who? Dale?'

His lip curls at the sound of his name. 'I've watched how he treats you and things are going to be so different now. You won't even need to work anymore. My wife's estate left me very well provided for.

'You never told me *how* she died.'

His expression changes as the question hangs between us for several moments and he looks away.

17

'SHE HIT HER HEAD.'

'And that *killed* her?.'

'Yes, but if you don't mind, it's a conversation I'd rather not pursue.' He shoves two chips into his mouth and chews as if this is a *normal* meal. As though he hasn't tricked me into being here with him. 'I want to talk about *us*.'

It's on the tip of my tongue to say, *there is no us,* but I'd better not inflame things again. He's settled down and I just need to play along until I get a chance to hunt for the key and my phone.

'You don't know how long I've waited for this day.' He rests his fork down and reaches across the table, brushing the tips of his fingers against mine. I edge my hand away and reach for the stalk of my glass, not that there's any chance of me raising it to my lips.

'Eat, Tamara.' His voice takes on a more urgent tone. 'I've been meaning to tell you for some time that you're way too thin.' His eyes are swimming with concern. 'I know it's been *you* who's been doing all the shopping and cooking up to now. Well,

I'm here to tell you all that's going to change. You deserve to be looked after.'

'I'm really not all that hungry.' My stomach churns as I stare at my barely touched meal. *How the hell can he expect me to eat?* 'I had a late lunch at work.'

'But it's your favourite.' He looks mildly hurt as he points at my plate.

Once again, I stab my fork into the meat and hack off another piece, the clatter of cutlery against crockery echoing around the silent kitchen as he does the same.

'Mmmm,' he exclaims. 'Delicious food, even if I do say so myself, Fine wine, amazing company. What more could a man ask for?'

I don't reply. Besides I'm chewing. And chewing. I point at my mouth and then jump from my chair, to head to the kitchen roll next to the sink. He'll know as well as I do there isn't an ounce of fat on this steak for me to encounter a chewy bit but hopefully, he's unlikely to challenge me.

He jumps up too but this time he doesn't get in my way. However, he's watching every move I make. I spit the meat into the towel and then lunge at a drawer, praying it's the drawer where knives are kept. There's a metallic rattle as it flies open. I only have a chance to glimpse the fact that it contains every other utensil apart from knives. Before he slams it shut.

'What are you looking for, Tamara?'

'Just a steak knife.' I give him my best wide-eyed look of innocence. I bet he's moved all the knives.

'Do you want me to cut it up for you?'

I shake my head. What does he think I am – three years old?

'Your food will be going cold.'

I retake my seat. I'll keep picking at my meal and hopefully soon, he'll need to excuse himself to visit the toilet.

'So—' I've got to take some control here. 'You clearly know lots about me, don't you? So how about you?'

'What do you mean?'

'Well, here we are, eating a meal together, but I know nothing about *you*.'

His eyes narrow. 'Well if you hadn't ignored me for all these years, perhaps you might. Instead, we've wasted all this time.'

'I haven't ignored you. You've freaked me out. And you're still freaking me out – telling me I look like your dead wife.'

His frown deepens. I'd better backpedal so I go on. 'Look, what's done is done. We're here now, aren't we?'

His expression mellows at that so I pick up my fork. Perhaps I can appease him further by getting a bit more of my food down. 'So what do *you* like, Martin?'

'You,' he replies. 'You're the only thing that brings meaning into my life – I must have proven that to you. I want to talk about *you*.'

'There's nothing much to say.'

'I've seen how unhappy you've been.'

'All marriages have their ups and downs.'

'You shouldn't be with him.' He rests his knife down next to his plate. 'I've heard the two of you arguing. I've watched how insecure he makes you. His affair—'

'That's over now.' I reach for my water. My heart is hammering against my chest. I can't eat this meal. I can't keep talking to this man. Somehow, I just need to get myself out of here. 'We moved house – it was supposed to be a new start.' My use of the word *supposed* will probably give Martin false hope but perhaps that isn't such a bad thing.

'I know exactly how it feels, you know.' His voice softens even more but he isn't taking his eyes off me. I've never been held in this much intensity of someone's gaze before and it's the most unnerved I've ever been. 'Me and you,' – he points from himself then to me, – 'have far more in common than you think.'

I stare down at my nails. Sian painted them in a glittery blue the other day. It was my hit back against Valentine's Day. I knew Dale wouldn't be offering any grand gestures and I could hardly bear to follow the masses of women in the salon, all requesting the red shades ahead of their romantic evenings out, so I went for the blue.

'Look at me, Tamara.'

Slowly, I raise my eyes to look into those of my captor.

'Belinda was having an affair too.'

'Belinda?'

'My wife.'

'Was she hit over the head by the man she was having an affair with?'

'She just didn't want to be with *me* anymore.' He pushes peas around his plate but seems about to tell me more. 'And her body was found at the bottom of Fewston reservoir.' He continues to stare down at his plate. 'A couple of months later.'

Belinda Sanders, *the woman in the water*. It was all over the local news at the time.

'You probably saw me on the news.' It's as if he's telepathic. 'When I pleaded for help to catch her killer and the police were warning other women not to be alone around the reservoir.'

'Did they ever find who did it?'

He shakes his head.

18

'IT'S ALRIGHT, Tamara. You can leave it if you want to.' He points at my plate, having eaten every morsel on his. How can he possibly have any appetite after kidnapping me?

I rest my cutlery across my uneaten food and clasp my hands in the lap of my unfamiliar dress. It felt wonderful when I first put it on but now it's scratchy and tight. I just want to be back in my own clothes. 'Like I said before, my stomach's off.'

'I'm not going to force you to eat,' he goes on, which also fills me with hope that if he's saying this, he won't try to force me into anything else. His broad chest and bulging biceps tell me I wouldn't stand a chance if he wanted to overpower me and a violation like that would probably hurt the baby. I glance around again for something to fight back with if he were to try anything.

I could hit him over the head with a chair but he looks so solid that even if he didn't raise an arm to block my attempt, the chair would just bounce off him like rainwater off a car roof. He's moved the wine bottle but I still have my glass. I could smash it on the edge of the table and then cut him somewhere nasty. But would it work? Somehow, I doubt it. The glass would either smash into smithereens on the floor or he'd restrain me before I could do any damage. Either way, I'd probably make things ten times worse for myself.

'I'm not some kind of monster, you know.' His voice cuts into my musings as though he can somehow sense what I'm thinking. 'I'm just someone who happens to be in love with you.' His lips curve into a smile and my stomach churns even harder.

'You might *think* you are, Martin.' It's the first time I've used his name. Perhaps it will elicit some trust from him towards me. 'But really, like I've already said, you hardly know me. You might have watched me but this is the first time we've actually spoken.'

'That's where you're wrong,' he replies. 'Honestly, I know you better than you know yourself.'

His words chill me to the core on so many levels. And I feel helpless and vulnerable, here at thirteen weeks pregnant, locked in where no one knows where I am, wearing a stupid dress and kitten heels. Why the hell haven't the police ever acted on my complaints? Or my husband and sister? The man's disturbed and it should *never* have come to this.

'And I love you a million times more than *he* ever could.' Martin's tone takes on that edge again. 'Anyway, let's not talk about him.' He stands from his chair, collects his plate in one hand and mine in the other and then strides over to the sink. 'I've got so many plans for us.' He scrapes my uneaten food into the bin. 'We've got lots to look forward to.'

I swallow hard. He's not going to let me go tonight by the sounds of it. How the hell am I going to get away from him?

'Why don't I wash the dishes?' *What I mean is let me at those drawers again.* There must be something in them – a corkscrew or a rolling pin, perhaps? I start getting to my feet but he grabs a tea towel and flies towards me, giving me a gentle tap on the shoulder to direct me back into my seat.

'I wouldn't hear of it. You're going to be looked after in the way you deserve to be looked after. Starting with...' He lunges to a cupboard door and pulls out a floppy soft toy. 'I was going to wait until later for all this but you look like you could do with cheering up *now*.'

'What the hell's that?' As if he's standing there with a furry squirrel thing clutching a heart with the words *I love you* across its belly. He sits it on the table in front of me. Things are going from the sublime to the ridiculous. 'I don't know what to say.'

'I won it for you at Filey.' He beams and his chest seems to swell with pride. 'While I've been waiting all this time for you, I've been storing up on the things we've been missing out on. And now we're together at last, there's nothing to stop me giving them all to you.'

I'm speechless as he pulls his next item from the cupboard. It's a DVD of *Me Before You.*

'I was sitting behind you in the cinema when you watched this,' he explains. 'I noticed you crying. I must admit, it brought a tear to my eye to see you. Anyway, we can enjoy it together now.'

'You were sitting *behind* me?' It's warm in this kitchen but I still shiver. That he was in such close proximity gives me goose-bumps. Surely I'd have been able to sense him so near to me? From what I'm gathering this evening, it seems the diary I've been keeping on him will be only the tip of the iceberg.

But there's no denying that a DVD *is* hopeful. If we were to move out of the kitchen and into the lounge, not only does it offer the chance for him to fall asleep after his meal, it also gives me another room to stake out. More places where he might have hidden my phone and the keys. I can also scan it for potential weapons. I need something that's guaranteed to completely immobilise him. It needs to be heavy, yet something

I can easily swing at him without hurting or straining my stomach.

I know one thing for certain. If we get out of here without him killing me or vice versa, he clearly needs psychiatric help. His fixation on me seems to be rooted in grief for his dead wife. If I can bring this realisation home to him, he might come to his senses and let me go.

'Did you have any counselling after losing your wife, Martin?'

His face darkens as he rests a CD on the counter. 'Here I am, trying to make up for all the time we've lost and *you—.*'

'I'm sorry.' Though it's almost impossible, I must keep playing along – it's the only way of disarming him. 'It's just that if we're to go forward together from now on, unless you properly deal with and talk about the loss of your wife, you risk—'

'I've had all the *counselling* I need.' His voice is clipped. 'Besides, all that matters to me now is the present and our future.'

'What do you mean?' I swallow. Any minute now I'm going to wake up from this. He has no plans whatsoever to let me go. I look around the kitchen again as if some means of escape will miraculously present itself.

'Like I say, I've got this place for as long as we want to stay here.' He sweeps his free arm around where he's standing. 'And look.' He reaches for the CD and holds it in front of me. 'I've compiled all your favourite songs and even printed a sleeve for it.' He turns the case over and I feel the weight of his stare on me. 'I bet *he* would never go to all this trouble for you.'

'But how would you—'

'I've been behind you in traffic, watching you sing.' He smiles, as though recalling a fond memory. He would honestly be a good-looking man if he wasn't so deranged. 'I've been in your garden, watching you dance around. I've been—'

'Alright. I get the picture.' From the wounded look he gives me, I realise my voice was probably too sharp.

'I'm sorry,' I say. 'It's just a lot to take in, that's all.'

All this time, I've been trying to convince Dale that someone was following me and he just treated me like I was going mad. He even had the gall to once blame his affair on my paranoia. *You'd have driven a monk to it*, he told me once in the throes of an argument. And even in our new house, where we were supposed to be having a fresh start, he's acted like he never wants to come home in the evening and rarely shows his face before eight o'clock. He's too busy with his precious gym. And, more than likely, the woman across the road.

Martin bends forward to continue with his cupboard of never-ending tricks.

'A dozen red roses.' He smiles. 'And there'll be plenty more where these came from.' He lays them in front of me, the cellophane and tissue paper crinkling with the movement. What I'd have given to have received these from my husband. 'I'll have to find something to put them in.' I swallow. A nice, heavy vase. Hopefully something I can clock him over the head with to buy me some time to find those keys and get out of here.

'Daisy Perfume. I know it's your favourite.' I swallow. God only knows how he's worked out what perfume I wear. I'll never wear it again after this.

'And I can't wait to see you in this little number.' He produces a bag marked *Victoria's Secret*. Oh my God, oh my God. His intentions are evidently going well beyond dinner.

'Don't worry.' He must notice my expression as he peels the outer layer of wrapping from the perfume box. 'We won't rush anything. Not until you're ready – it's really important to me that you're ready. After all, we're here, alone, and we've got all the time in the world.' He opens the box lid and slides the bottle out.

'But.' The vision of the same bottle I keep on my dressing

table with its ornate flower lid is almost comforting. 'How long are you intending to keep me here exactly?' I've asked the question but don't really want to hear the answer.

He beckons for me to hold my wrist out. I do as instructed and he sprays the perfume onto it, the floral scent filling my nostrils.

'This is us now. Our old lives are over.'

19

HE POINTS AT MY NECK. 'I'm going to make you more happy than you've ever known.'

'But my business—'

'I've already sent a note to your salon. They'll get it in the morning.'

'What?'

'I've signed it from you telling them you won't be back for the foreseeable future.'

'What are you talking about? I can't just *not go back.*' The man's even crazier than I thought. I allow him to spray my neck, the fragrance inviting fresh tears to my eyes. I wore this perfume on my wedding day. It used to be a happy scent.

'You smell beautiful.' He clicks the lid back onto the bottle. 'I can't tell you how good it feels for us to finally be close and properly together, instead of all the watching and longing for you from a distance.' He licks his lips. 'At last, those days are over.'

I look for a bulge in his pockets where a bunch of keys might be but there's nothing. I'm going to have to wait for him to fall asleep. We can't just go on like this *all* night. He'll have to fall asleep *sooner or later*.

'And now.' He produces a ring box from the cupboard which he holds lightly between his fingers. 'We might as well make things official. These are *yours* now and I want you to wear them.'

'What are they?' I twist my rings around on my wedding finger, while I try to telepathise to my husband. *I'm in trouble – please try to find me.* At least I've still got my rings. I couldn't help but feel that Dale lost his wedding ring on purpose when he claimed to not be able to find it.

'You can swap those over for these now.' He points at my ring finger before opening the box to reveal a white gold wedding band and a diamond solitaire engagement ring. 'Your fingers look to be a similar size to Belinda's. At least now they'll be worn by the woman who should have had them all along.'

'I can't wear another woman's wedding rings.' I hold my hands behind my back. Over my dead body will he get those onto my finger. The very idea makes my flesh crawl.

'They're yours now.' His wounded expression returns as he rests his hand on the top of my arm. I'm *not* taking the rings I've worn for fourteen years off. Who knows what he'll do with them? 'Please, Tamara. It would mean the world to me.' He twirls the rings around in between his fingers. 'Take those things off.'

We continue to stare at each other for a moment.

'You're making me feel just like *she* used to. Please, Tamara, I thought you were different from her.' His voice is a cross between menace and desperation.

I swallow. 'You mean Belinda?' He mentioned before about how her body ended up in the reservoir. Is that what he intends for me if I don't make him feel as he wants to feel? I glance down at his hands, the veins in the one which still rests on my arm protruding. His other hand is outstretched, waiting for me to drop my precious rings into his palm. What if I give them to him? What if I never see them again? Yes, my marriage is in trouble but I'm sure it can still be fixed.

'Take your rings off, Tamara. Please.' His breathing sounds like it's coming faster.

I bring my hands to the front of my chest, shaking his hand off me in the process, and I make an exaggerated mock effort to pull them off. 'It's warm in here,' I say. 'I can only get them to my knuckle. They're stuck.'

'You don't look like you're trying hard enough.' He has a wild look in his eyes which suggests he'll take an axe to my finger if it comes to it.

Finally, I slip them off but curl my fingers around them. 'Right, I've got them off but *I'm* keeping hold of them.'

'Give them to me.' He thrusts his shovel-sized palm closer to me.

'I can't.' I begin to back away but there's not far for me to go before I'm backed into a cupboard door. 'I didn't pay for them. I can't just—'

'Give me the rings.' He pursues me to the cupboard. I'm going to have to hand them over. Who knows what might happen if I don't?

I uncurl my fingers, watching as the overhead light catches the diamond in my ring. This might be the last time I ever see it.

The tips of his fingers tickle my palm as he scoops them up before lurching to the sink. I nearly choke on my sob as he drops them into the plughole and rinses some water down after them.

'That's the end of those then.' He holds his wife's rings in front of me. 'Give me your hand.'

'I don't want to.' The bastard really is about to force me to wear his dead wife's rings. This could be her dress I'm wearing. Her stockings, her underwear, her shoes. There were no shop labels in any of the things I put on. The thought of being dressed head to toe in the clothing of a woman six years dead is a sickening one.

'Why are you being like this, Tamara?'

I have no choice but to offer my hand which shakes uncontrollably as he slides each ring onto it, before raising it to his mouth and pressing my finger against his lips.

'You must never take them off.'

The slime of his mouth against my skin makes me shudder.

'I can't tell you how happy you've made me,' he murmurs as he steps right up to me. His stagnant breath is in my face before I realise what he's about to do.

'No.' I push him, surprising myself at the force with which he staggers back. 'I'm not ready for any of that. I've only just met you.'

His startled expression becomes hurt, then fury, then back to hurt again. He looks to be trying to compose himself.

'You're going to have to come with me to the little boys' room.' Grabbing my shoulder again, he spins me around and begins frogmarching me towards the kitchen door. 'I don't think I can trust you to wait for me down here.'

Horror creeps over me.

20

'JUST STAND THERE.' He points at the heated towel rail as he closes the door. 'You don't have to watch.' I turn to face it. The last thing I want to see is him at the toilet.

He begins to pee, the stench of his urine in the claustrophobic bathroom making me gag.

However, while he's otherwise engaged, I've got a chance to get away. I might strike it lucky straightaway and stumble straight across his hiding place for my things or the keys. I bolt for the door and am just about to make a run toward the bedroom when he spins from where he's pointing at the toilet in mid-flow, spraying me with his piss.

'Now look what you made me do.'

I make it to the bedroom but no sooner have I swept my gaze over the room than he's behind me. I spin around and scream as he comes towards me while zipping himself up.

'No.' I back away. I can't be cornered in the bedroom with him, especially after the underwear he produced from the cupboard downstairs. What if he tries to rape me? I won't let him. I'll twist his bollocks off first. 'Please, Martin, I'm sorry, I just wanted to find my things.'

'Why do you keep trying to spoil everything?'

'Let's go back downstairs.' My words pump out as gasps. 'Let's have another drink.'

'Will you actually drink it this time?'

'Yes, but, I need to change my clothes.'

'You won't be wearing your old clothes again. Besides, I picked that dress out, especially for you. For tonight.' The man's even madder than I thought.

'But I'm soaked with your—'

'It was an accident,' he cuts in. 'Your trying to run off like that caught me by surprise.'

'I need the toilet as well.' At the very least I can towel myself off and have a bit of a wash in there if he lets me go.

'I'll tell you what. You can have the clothes that are meant for tomorrow. He points at a folded pile on the bed. But I'll have to keep an eye on you while you're in the bathroom.'

No way. 'Can't you just wait outside for me? You did before. It's not as if I can get anywhere else from there, is it?'

'I'm sorry, Tamara. I'm just not sure I can trust you. It's a shame really. I'd hoped your looks and way of talking were your only similarities to Belinda.'

I tug the dress as far down my legs as possible while I pee, looking down at the spray of his urine across the floor as the light above us shines onto it. It's preferable to look at that rather than at the probable leer on his face. I don't know where or how this is going to end. And I've never had *anyone* watch me on the toilet before.

'Please – just turn the other way, at least.' But he doesn't. Instead, he continues to watch intently. I tug the knickers he chose back over myself and flush. The man's not just a deluded, stalking weirdo, it also seems he's a pervert. Usually, I check my knickers for blood when visiting the loo. But I can't this time. Not with him standing there.

He passes me the jumper and jeans. Judging from the slight fraying on the hem of the jeans, they definitely aren't new. More items from his dead wife, I suspect.

'Please look the other way.'

He doesn't. I tug the jeans over my knickers and stockings but under the cover of my dress and then turn away as I pull it over my head, grimacing as the piss patch brushes against my face. The jumper scratches my skin but at least I'm out of that dress.

'Would you like more wine, Tamara?' He points to a spot on the kitchen floor. 'Stand there while I get the bottle.'

'Can we go through to the lounge and make ourselves more comfortable?' I ask. If he gets enough of that wine down his neck, he'll eventually pass out. Everyone needs sleep eventually – even psychotic maniacs.

As he briefly turns his back, I tilt my watch towards my face. It's been over three hours since the Uber dropped me off. I wonder what Dale's doing. Will he have done *anything* to find me? Will he have even *attempted* to contact me? Or has he hot-footed it over to that bitch of a neighbour's house? A vision of them kissing swims into my mind and I blink it away. I can't think about all that now – I have to focus on getting myself out of this horrendous predicament I've found myself in. Perhaps it's karma. Maybe I'm never going to get out of it.

He doesn't answer my question so I reframe it. 'We could watch that film together – if there's a DVD player in the lounge?'

I can't believe what I'm suggesting but if he agrees to put the film on, I will have bought myself ninety minutes to work out how I'm going to get out of here. It will be ninety minutes of him drinking more wine and hopefully becoming sleepier. Unless he's thrown the keys and my phone from a window, they've got to be here *somewhere*. Until I find them, I won't leave a single place unchecked.

21

THE TWO GLASSES he's carrying clank against the wine bottle as he uses his other hand to guide me into the lounge. I head to the armchair nearest the fire but he points at the sofa. 'No –sit there. We're a couple now, aren't we?'

He throws coals from the bucket onto the fire. There's a bloody fire. So there must be some tools to maintain it and to keep the fireplace clean. However, he's probably moved them.

If only the coals were stored in a traditional brass coal scuttle. It could have doubled up as something I could have hit him over the head with. Instead, they're in a plastic bucket. I can't do much damage with that.

He sits beside me in the dimly lit room, his leg touching mine. I shift mine away and point at the DVD player. 'Are you going to put the film on?'

'To be honest, I'd rather talk than watch a film.' I tense up as he reaches for my hand and brushes his slimy lips once again across the rings he's forced me to wear. 'We've got so many missed years to make up for.'

I tug my hand away. 'Are you going to pour the wine?' I could do with something I can inhale while I'm sitting here, even though I've no intention of drinking it. Something that smells better than what still lingers on my skin. It's completely overpowered the perfume he sprayed on me before.

'Of course.' As he turns the glasses over on the coffee table beside him and wine begins to glug into the first glass, I shiver in the clothes he's given me, thinking of the stretchy leggings and cosy hoodie that are packed in my holdall. What I wouldn't give to have been able to carry out my original plan of booking somewhere to give me some space and to hopefully make Dale miss me and bring him to his senses. How the hell have I ended up in this situation?

'Are you cold, sweetheart? Tuck yourself into me.' He rests the bottle down and raises his arm, wrapping it around me and drawing me into him as I scrunch my eyes together in disgust. 'We can't be having that.' He smells of aftershave and wine but still, the overriding stench in here is the urine he's squirted all over me. My damp hair is still clinging to my neck and if I think about it too hard, I'll just throw up.

'Actually, I'll sit by the fire for a few minutes if you don't mind.' I rock from the sofa and then drop down onto the rug by the fire before he can prevent me. 'I need to get warmed up.'

'I'll join you then.' He does the same and suddenly we're facing each other, our faces lit by the flames that are beginning to lick at the fresh coals he's put on. 'Well this is romantic, isn't it?'

To think I thought this would be Dale and me tonight. Together, on a secluded Valentine's getaway, putting our marriage right and carefully placing our stepping stones for the future.

'I'm so happy to see you wearing those rings.' He nods towards my left hand. 'I can't believe they fit you so well. They were obviously meant for you.'

I follow his gaze to my hand. 'Did they ever find out who dumped her in the water, Martin?' My voice is soft as I raise my eyes to meet his. I know they *didn't*. I remember it being on Crimewatch UK. Her family all begging for anyone with information to come forward. Her tearful husband, now sitting facing me. I recall him pleading for the public's help to bring his wife's killer to justice.

'Belinda was having an affair,' he tells me again, as though that should explain things.

'And?'

His nose wrinkles, portraying his disgust at the memories that are being stirred up. 'She was *mine*, not his.'

'These things happen, Martin. Just like they have to me.' I pick at some loose fibres on the rug. The rug where I might end my days if I put a foot wrong.

'She was *mine*.' His voice hardens. 'Just like *you* are now. But she pushed me too far.'

His face crumples and he drops his head into his hands. While he's not looking, my eyes dart around the room. There's no such thing as a coal fire without a poker. If I could only find it. It would be small and light enough not to put any strain on my uterus, but just one hard swing at his head would be enough to disable him. And if it wasn't, I could be straight back for a second go.

'Belinda's memory has been completely sullied by her betrayal.' His eyes shine with tears as he lifts his head.

'You mean her affair?'

'I caught her with him. The cowardly bastard ran off but then it all got out of hand with Belinda.' Tears are leaking from his eyes.

'What do you mean?'

'She wouldn't wake up.' His words are wobbling. 'I shouted at her. I even slapped her. I slapped her again and again but she still wouldn't wake up.'

An image of this brute standing over a corpse which he repeatedly slapped invites bile to bubble at the base of my throat. It's Valentine's night and here I am sitting on a rug in front of a fire with a psycho. I'm shaking from the inside out, despite the fire that's starting to take hold and the warmth that's wafting around. At the moment he seems calm and fairly meek but that could easily change without warning.

'It was all my fault.' His bottom lip is trembling but his eyes don't leave mine. 'I didn't mean for it to happen, I swear to you.' His voice is a husk.

'Was it *you* who left her in the water?' He hasn't actually confirmed this to me yet. I won't use the words weighed down and dumped which were used in the news reports. If it hadn't been for her sister's tireless campaigning that Belinda couldn't possibly have just *left* without telling anyone, perhaps the police might have stopped looking earlier. There was no evidence to suggest anything sinister had happened in her home, no witnesses, no CCTV. She could have just gone off somewhere. After all, people do.

Her body had been in such an awful state of decomposition when it was found, they could only give an approximation of how long it might have been there. It was concluded that she'd been attacked on the public footpath of the reservoir, before meeting her watery grave.

Will Ali do the same for me if I meet a similar fate to Belinda tonight? Will she ensure I'm hunted for until I'm found? Surely she will. I'm supposed to be babysitting for my nephews tomorrow. In the thick of everything that's happened over the last twenty-four hours, I completely forgot about that. If I can just hang on and somehow dance to the tune of this maniac, by tomorrow, she'll be looking for me.

He nods. 'I honestly didn't think they'd ever find her. It's a deep reservoir. But it was hot that year.'

'I know.' I used to enjoy walking around there in the summer but I haven't stepped foot near it since. I might never step *anywhere* again if he kills me off. The water had dipped to critical levels that year and the hosepipe ban had been extended. Had the water levels not been as low as they got, perhaps Belinda would *never* have been found.

'And they interviewed you?'

I already know they did as I took an interest in the reporting at the time. Everyone's sympathy was with *the husband*. Then everyone, including me, held their breath while he was 'helping the police with their enquiries.' Until they released him without charge. Women in the locality were careful for a while and never walked alone around the reservoir, just in case. But eventually, Belinda's memory became yesterday's chip paper.

'Of course they did. But they never had anything to charge me with. I live in a converted farmhouse with no other houses nearby so I could get her into the boot easily enough. And it was pitch black at the reservoir so nobody was around.'

It's the stuff of horror films and if I don't do something drastic, I'm set to be the next woman bundled into his boot. There wasn't a car at the front when I arrived, for him to transport me – there was barely any space for one. However, this style of cottage often has its parking space around the back.

'Didn't they check your car? There must have been fibres, or her hair or blood. Or something.'

'Of course they did.' He pauses, as though deliberating whether to tell me any more.

'What?'

'I'd wrapped her in some plastic sheeting from some flooring we'd had delivered. So there was no trace of her in my car. Other than, of course, in the driver and passenger seats where she'd drove and rode.'

It sounds like Martin had plenty of time to cover his tracks. And for six years, as far as he knows at the moment, he's got away with his wife's murder.

22

'It's a relief to finally talk about it,' he continues. 'What I did has weighed me down more than you could ever know.'

The irony of his words isn't lost on me.

'She shouldn't be dead.' He stares down at his hands. 'I'm not an evil man, Tamara. You know that, don't you? Things just went too far, that's all.'

I can't take my eyes from his hands. How am I going to stop them ending up around my neck? He's already proven he'll stop at nothing to prevent me leaving. The frustration and hopelessness of being trapped in this house is gnawing at my insides. Something's got to give soon. My skin is crawling with fear and hatred.

'Are you planning to do the same to me next?' I have to know if that's why he's lured *me* here. If he's planning the same endgame for me. The same final resting place.

'You're going to save me, Tamara. With *you*, I've got another chance and I can make amends for what I've done. Tonight is only the beginning of the rest of our lives.'

'But I've got to look after my nephews tomorrow.' My words sound lame but he clearly needs a reminder that I'm *not* a reincarnation of his wife and that I have my own life beyond the walls he's imprisoned me in. 'I promised. I could come back here afterwards.' My words are laughable but he doesn't laugh. Far from it.

'I can't believe you're trying to get away from me. I honestly thought you wanted this as much as I do.'

'At least let me tell my sister that I can't help with the kids. She'll be trying to get hold of me. She might even come looking if she doesn't hear anything.'

'She won't find you here. In any case, your life is with *me* now, not your sister and certainly not *him*. Here. Where it's just me and you. Where I can take care of you if you'll let me. I really thought you'd be happier to be here than you've been so far.'

'Just give me my phone, Martin, please, just for a moment. Let me send a quick message to my sister. You can even watch me type it.' I'll put something in the text that she'll query. I'm renowned for sending perfectly punctuated, lengthy texts so if I send something that's the complete opposite or even just get the chance to quickly type the word *help,* she'll be on alert and looking for me straight away.

'There is no phone.' The wild look has returned to his eyes. 'I'm really sorry but I had to destroy it.'

I should have known. I'll never know whether Dale has tried to find me. Not unless I get the chance to see him again. My only hope is finding those bloody keys. I haven't heard a single car go up or down the lane since I was dropped off here. Maybe tomorrow, when it's light, walkers might be around. If I can make it until tomorrow. I stare down at the rug. I've got to do *something* but I've never been more terrified in my life.

'So what now?' I break the deadlock between us.

'I'm hoping we can head up to bed. Like any normal husband and wife would.' He points at my rings.

'How do you mean?' I don't really need to ask this but I'm

playing for time. This is insane. He's insane. And his mood has changed direction so many times, I can't possibly preempt what might come next. 'You said you weren't going to rush me into anything.'

The calm between us is growing heavier. I *have* to do something. No way am I going to risk him forcing himself onto me.

'I wasn't going to tell you this but I'm three months pregnant, Martin. With my husband's baby.' My hand falls protectively onto my belly. Perhaps I should have told him this from the off. He might have let me go straightaway. 'That's why I haven't drunk my wine.'

His face twists into an expression that's a cross between disbelief and anger. 'Why the hell didn't you tell me?'

'I was scared you might do something to hurt it.' I edge away from him.

'I've already told you I'm not a monster.' But the way he grits his teeth and cracks one of his knuckles suggests otherwise. My news has seriously rattled him.

'So now you know, will you let me go?'

'Is this some kind of elaborate lie, Tamara?' His face is white and pinched. 'You wouldn't lie to me, would you?'

'Of course not. I haven't really told anyone about the baby yet. It's still very early days, and—'

'You're not the person I thought you were. In fact, you're even more like *she* was than I first thought. You've been wanting to get away from me since you arrived. You even look at me with the same disgust she did.'

'I'm just me.' A tear rolls down my face and drips onto my arm. 'Tamara. I'm not Belinda.'

He rocks up onto his knees, closing the gap between us. 'I never planned to hurt you. I didn't want anything else on my conscience.' He wipes at his cheek with the back of his hand.

More tears leak from my eyes. I'm crying for my baby, for the life it might never get to live by the sounds of it. And also for the life I haven't lived to the full so far – the life that he may be about to end. All because he thinks I look like her.

'I thought bringing us together like this would be enough.' He edges closer. 'But now you've told the truth about *that*,' – he points at my stomach, – 'I really don't know what to do for the best.' He sighs. 'You haven't left me with many choices really.'

'What do you mean?' I glance at the coal bucket. Maybe a well-placed whack on the side of the head with a lump of coal might do the trick. Though probably not. It would be more likely to crumble against the side of his skull.

'I really don't want to hurt you, Tamara.' He swings his legs out and hauls himself to his feet. 'Stand up.' He offers his hand.

I weep harder, with relief that he hasn't killed me yet and with fear of what he might be about to do. Why is this happening to me? Why now?

He yanks me to my feet as though I weigh nothing. I suppose, compared to him, I don't. 'Come with me.'

Surely if he was going to force himself on me he wouldn't be leading me up to the bedroom to do it. He's got the size and strength just to pin me down on the rug. 'Where are we going? What are you going to do to me?'

I let a long breath out as he steers me past the bottom of the stairs and back into the kitchen. The air is still thick with the smell of our meal, a smell which turns my stomach. But at least he isn't forcing me back upstairs.

'Please, Martin, if you just let me go, I won't breathe a word to anyone about any of this. We can pretend it never happened and both get on with our lives.'

'You're not going back to *him*.' He pulls a door open which I thought was a cupboard. However, the darkness beyond it tells a different story. 'But after your *news*, I need time to work out what I'm going to do. I need to think.'

'What is it? What's in there?' I cling to the doorframe as he tries to manoeuvre me inside.

'It's a cellar. What do you think it is? You'll have to watch yourself on the steps.'

He releases his hold on me and it seems I have two choices. Try to fight my way back past him and risk being thrown down the steps he's just referred to, or go in willingly and look for a way out down there. Cellars have gaps, air vents, some even have their own entrances.

'Please, at least give me my coat. I'll freeze down there.'

'I don't want to do this but you've left me with no alternative. I can't bear to look at you right now.'

'I thought you said you loved me. I could *die* if you just leave me.'

'Get in there, Tamara.'

He's pushing me more forcibly. As the door bangs behind me and the key turns in the lock, I lose my footing on the top step in the darkness. My arms flail out to steady myself but it's no good. My nails scratch against the concrete as I hurtle down the rest of them.

23

I BLINK in the darkness and it takes a moment for me to make any sense of how I've come to be sprawled on a freezing concrete floor. I try to raise my head but it hurts too much. I must have banged it on the way down. I wriggle my fingers and toes, then my wrists and ankles. I raise my hand to my head. My hair feels matted and sticky but other than that, nothing else seems to be badly hurt. Until I remember...

My baby.

My head swoons as I sit upright, my hand flying to my belly. 'Please be alright, please be alright.' I reach inside the jeans and into the knickers that don't belong to me, feeling for the thick, syrupy pool within them that would indicate another loss is taking place. 'Please no, please no.' They're dry. I stroke my midriff, the movement generating the slightest amount of warmth. 'You must be made of tough stuff. Just like your mum.' I kiss the palm of my hand and press it to my belly. The baby seems to be safe. That's the main thing.

Tears warm my cheeks as I try to work out where I am and how I got here. Then it all comes flooding back. It was bad enough when he thought he had just *me* trapped here but now he knows about the baby as well.

If he planned to either rape or kill me, or both, surely he'd have done it by now? Unless dragging it out and making me suffer is all part of his game. I have to hang onto the remorse in his words when he confessed about his wife.

But by his own admission, it all went too far. And it's going too far now as well.

Oh God, what am I thinking here? I'm almost making excuses for him. And I'm going to be next in that watery grave if I don't do *something*. Shivering, I haul myself first to my knees then to my stockinged feet.

I feel around the damp wall for a light switch. My stomach sags in relief as I find and flick it. Shit. It's not bloody working.

I can't see a thing around me. There could be huge spiders down here, or even rats. I tremble even more violently and not just with the cold. I rub at the sides of my arms with my numb hands. You couldn't make it up. But I've got to keep going. What's worse. Encountering a rat or facing that maniac.

I slide my foot in a circle around the vicinity of where I'm standing to check I'm not going to stand on anything or trip, holding onto the wall as I make my way around the edge of the cellar. Concrete crumbles beneath my fingers with every touch as I continue feeling my way around the walls, looking for anything loose, any gaps at the top, any hope of escaping.

But there's nothing. Being out in the countryside means that even if there are any gaps at the top of the walls, it's so dark out there, there'll be no light. And it's been cloudy all week, so the moon's been barely visible. I suppose I should be glad of the cloud cover. If we had clear skies I'd be more likely to freeze to death.

Maybe, eventually, he'll relent and throw my coat down to me. Or let me out completely. I really can't see him letting me go from here now, especially after what he's told me. There might be only one way out of this place for me – inside a body bag.

I can't believe I've been reduced to this, grovelling around a pitch-black cellar. Just as I'm giving up hope of finding anything to help me, my hands come to a pile of what feels like broken-up boxes. At least I'll have something to lie on if I end up in here all night. *All night.* It's almost unthinkable but it's a definite possibility.

I tilt my watch towards me. I've either broken it in the fall or it ran out of charge. Whatever it is, I've no idea of the time or how long I've been out of it after tumbling down those steps. Really, I need to get to a hospital. I *have* to know if the baby's alright.

I arrange some of the boxes on the ground and against the wall before sliding into a crouch. My head hurts so badly that I can't remain upright any longer. I close my eyes, frantically trying to assemble my jumbled thoughts. Dale won't be looking for me. The girls at the salon won't be looking for me. My only hope is Ali and since she's expecting me to babysit tomorrow, she won't rest until she finds me – I know she won't. I can't give up – I've got to believe someone will come looking.

My fingers land on something softer than the unforgiving concrete I'm surrounded by. It could be cloth sacks. I let a long breath of relief out. Once the pain in my head eases, I can keep periodically moving about and then when I have to stop and rest, I've got the sacks and the cardboard. Somehow I'll get us out of this hellhole. I've got to. My baby's depending on me.

He's moving about up there. A door which sounds like the dishwasher bangs. How can he so nonchalantly carry on after imprisoning me in here? Especially now he knows I'm pregnant. It would make most men more protective but with him, it's definitely gone the other way.

I wish I had some idea of what he could be planning to do with me, however, I don't think he has any sort of plan. Somewhere in his warped mental state, he thought he could just trap me in this house with him and I'd magically become what and who he wanted.

Oh my God, he's put the TV on. As if nothing's happened. As if he hasn't forced me into this cellar. At least this means he isn't going to just leave the house. If he leaves me locked down here, I've got no chance, I'll either freeze or starve to death. It could be days until my sister manages to find me. *If* she manages to find me.

I have to cling to the hope I've got. Once she looks for me at the salon, the girls will be able to tell her I left there in a taxi. All she's got to do is ring around the taxi firms and perhaps she'll even begin with Uber. They'll have a record of bringing me here. She'll find me – I know she will.

But what if she doesn't?

Panic overwhelms me as I try to get more breath in. It's so cold, each breath feels like a jagged knife within my lungs. I can't stay down here. Somehow, I've got to persuade him to let me back into the house where at least it's warm. I stagger to my feet, ignoring the pain in my head as I feel my way back around to the steps.

Still holding onto the wall, I begin ascending them as my heart hammers inside my chest. But there's no light visible beneath the door when I get to the top. It's like he's forgotten I'm down here. I bang on the door.

'Please Martin. Let me out. I'm hurt. I've fallen. I've been unconscious.' I bang again.

'Martin, I know my news has come as a shock to you and I'm sorry.' I rest my head against the door. 'I should have told you sooner.'

He doesn't reply but he's turned the volume down on the TV.

'Are you there? Can you hear me? Look, I promise things will be different if you just let me out. We can sit in front of the fire and watch that film together.' My teeth are chattering as I speak. What I'd give to be in front of that fire again. But he's still not responding. I need to change tack.

'Martin, listen to me. I'm sorry. I've been so ungrateful when you've been amazing.'

Why won't he answer me? The bastard.

'No one's ever looked after me like you have since I arrived. We can make this work but please, you've got to let me out of this cellar.'

Still silence. But I think he's in the kitchen now. I can sense his presence at the other side of the door. I swallow, steeling myself for the tripe I'm about to say to him. Desperate times call for more desperate measures.

'Listen to me, Martin. Please! You were right to lock me down here for a while. It's given me time alone to think and I've realised I love *you* too. I'm sure we can make this work. Perhaps we could be really happy. Me, you and the baby. We could pretend it's yours.'

A door bangs. Where the hell has he gone? What if he's left the cottage?

What if he's left me here to die?

PART II

24

ALI

I PULL up behind Dale's car, tugging the handbrake on just as my phone rings. I hurry to answer it in case it's my sister, however, it's my husband.

'You never said you were going out.'

'I shouted up the stairs to you,' I reply. 'Sorry, I thought you'd heard me.'

'Where are you anyway?'

'I'm just outside Tamara's. I needed to make sure she's alright.'

'You mean you need to make sure she's alright to babysit?' Wayne laughs. 'It's good to know you're looking forward to our night away.'

'Well there is that, and that's what she'll probably think when she opens the door, but the truth is that I'm also worried.' I glance into my mirror, noticing how much like my mother I look with my deepening frown lines.

'Because of that stalker story?'

'It's really got to her, Wayne, and she's banged on about it so many times that there must be *something* going on.'

'You've joked yourself about her overactive imagination.

Plus, like we were saying last night, she's not really been herself for the last couple of years.'

'All because of *Dale*.' I raise my eyes to the still-closed curtains of their house, just visible through the morning mist. I've never told Tamara what I *really* think of my brother-in-law. She's got to come to her own conclusions without my interference. 'Clearly, she's still got further lessons to learn from him.'

'There's no doubt her getting pregnant will have complicated things.'

'She'll leave him eventually. I can hardly imagine him winning any awards for *Dad of the Year*. He's never at home.'

'Why are you at her *house* anyway – wouldn't she be at the salon on a Saturday?'

'Yeah, I went there first but they told me she's gone away with Dale for the weekend but it's strange—'

Wayne tries to interrupt me with something but I keep talking over him.

'—both their cars are here, and in any case, I really can't see her leaving me in the lurch when she's agreed to have the boys. She knows it's a special anniversary for us and she's promised for ages—'

'She *can't* be away with Dale, love.' Wayne's voice carries the trace of an apology.

'What makes you say that?' My frown in the rear-view mirror deepens.

He lets a long breath out. 'Look, I was keeping this until after our night away as I didn't want to cause any drama but—' He hesitates.

'Just tell me, Wayne.' *Oh God, what now?* Things have been reasonably calm for too long. There's always something.

'Well, you know when I met my Dad for a pint last night?'

'Yes?'

'Dale was in the pub.'

I turn my mind back to last night, trying to determine when

Wayne left the house. Was it early enough that Dale could have gone off somewhere with Tamara *after* visiting the pub?

No, it can't have been. Wayne meets his Dad at eight o'clock, sharp. Ever since his Mum died, it's become their weekly ritual. Two pints and a catch-up. It's the second highlight of my father-in-law's week. The first is when he comes for dinner every Sunday and the boys are bribed into getting off their screens and giving him their undivided attention for a couple of hours.

'Did the two of you speak when you saw him?'

'Erm, no – he scarpered as soon as he clapped eyes on me and Dad.' His voice dips. 'Look Ali, there's no easy way of saying this so I'm just going to come out with it – our dear brother-in-law's up to his old tricks. He was with someone.'

'What do you mean, *someone*?' A cold dread creeps over me as I consider how Tamara will react. She doesn't need any more stress at the moment, not with the baby. 'A woman?'

'I'm afraid so. They were all over each other. Until Dale clocked me, watching them. They even left their drinks unfinished in their hurry to get away.'

'It must be this neighbour – the one she's been suspicious about.' I turn my head in the other direction, to the house straight across from my sister's. 'Poor Tamara. And I told her the other night that she risked driving Dale away if she kept acting so insecure.'

'Oh, Ali, you didn't tell her that, did you? After all she's been through with him?'

'I just wanted to snap her out of her miserable thinking.' It's my turn to sigh. 'I honestly didn't think he'd be capable of carrying on behind her back *again*. Especially not now they've got the baby on the way. Besides, it's only been a year since the last time.'

'Remind me not to come to *you* when I have a problem.' Wayne laughs.

'Don't. I feel bad enough for being so dismissive, but I

honestly thought she was just working herself up over nothing.'
I look at the house again, at the window my sister would have been standing at the other night when she was on the phone with me. 'I should have been more sympathetic.'

'How are you going to handle it now?'

'Who knows? I've given her the same advice over and over again for years and she never listens. She's got to come to her own senses that he's a liar and a cheat.'

'Are you going to confront him *now*? If he's even there, I mean.'

'I'm not sure – all the curtains are closed at their house, and the blinds are also down at the neighbour's. To be honest, something feels off.'

'Hmm, yes – it's after ten. Tamara's usually an early bird, isn't she?'

'I'm going to try her phone again before I go in,' I say. 'And that's another thing, she never switches it off. Ever. Even when she's in the middle of a salon treatment, she leaves it on silent. Not only that, four of my texts have gone unanswered. It's not like her at all.'

'It sounds like you'd better get to that door.'

'I know. I probably won't say anything to Tamara straight-away – I'll give him the chance to explain himself first – no doubt he'll try and slime out of what he's doing to my sister.'

'You'll know how to handle it – just keep me posted, love. Oh, and I'll get my dad on standby for having the kids tonight. They'll run him ragged but I'm sure he'll survive.'

'Good idea.' The last thing I want to do is foist my two on my increasingly frail father-in-law but with all that's blowing up here, Tamara's going to be in no fit state to keep her promise if she's found out about Dale. And I don't want to cancel. Wayne and I haven't had a night away on our own for so long and I've really been looking forward to our lovely spa hotel.

But first, I need to make sure my sister's alright.

25

ALI

THE CAR LOCKS with a beep and I head up Tamara's drive. The street is swathed in silence. I guess on this foggy February day, everyone's huddled inside their houses keeping cosy. That's normally what I'd be doing on a Saturday morning, curled up with a brew and a book while the boys are out at football practice.

As I thread my way past my sister's car, I suddenly notice why she won't have tried driving it. Her front tyre is as flat as a pancake. *And* her back tyre. Wait – all four of them are the same. I bend down. They're not just flat – bloody hell – they've been slashed. I glance back over at the neighbour's house. Could *she* have done this to Tamara? After all, I don't even want to consider the only other possible explanation.

I press the doorbell and wait. Nobody comes. I creep around to the lounge window, looking for gaps in the curtains. Nothing. I try the doorbell again. There's someone inside. I'm almost *certain* I just saw movement on the other side of the frosted glass. So why isn't she coming to the door?

'Tamara,' I call through the letter box. 'It's me – why aren't you answering?'

Silence. I try the door handle, which is what I should have done when I first arrived. To my amazement, the door's unlocked. I push it open and step inside the hallway. Dale appears in the kitchen doorway wearing boxers, a t-shirt and an expression of shock. His hair's on end as though he hasn't been long out of bed. 'What are *you* doing here?'

'What do you think – I'm looking for my sister.' There's a sudden movement in the kitchen behind where he's standing. 'Tamara?' I call out as I close the front door.

'She's not here.'

'So who *is* then?' I barge past my brother-in-law and fury snakes up my spine. Some buxom blonde in a dressing gown is sitting at my sister's kitchen table like she owns the place. 'Who the hell are you?'

'Look, this isn't what it looks like.' Dale rubs at the back of his neck. 'Rachel was just—'

'Oh, I can see exactly what *Rachel* has been doing.' I stride across the kitchen and tug at the back of her chair to tip her from it. 'Get out of my sister's house, do you hear me? Right now!'

She has no choice other than to stand from her chair as I continue to rock it forward. 'I'm going nowhere unless Dale asks me to leave.'

'You're nothing but a bastard.' I stare back at my brother-in-law still framed in the doorway, but looking like a deer caught in some car headlights. 'Haven't you cheated on Tamara enough? You make me sick.' I spin back around to look at the woman. 'And haven't you gone yet? Go on, get back to your own house. I take it this is the tart from over the road.' I point in that direction.

'Call me, Dale.' She stands with her hands on her hips but makes no move to follow my instruction. 'When you've got rid of this mad bitch.' She pulls a face as though *I'm* the person who's caused all the problems.

'Don't you dare call me names.' I grab her by the scruff of her dressing gown, that's if it's *her* dressing gown and not Tamara's.

'Ali, for God's sake.' Dale darts over to us, but he's too late as I march her backwards and ram her up against the door to the utility room.

'We women should stick together,' I shout into her face. 'Not go around pinching each other's husbands.'

'Ladies, please.' Dale's trying to prise us apart.

'She's no lady.'

'He came to *me*,' she smiles.

'You rotten bitch.' I let her go and push her away. 'As if you have the nerve to smile at me. Go home,' I continue, more calmly now. I'm not dealing with *her*. There are far more important things to sort out. 'I want to speak to my brother-in-law in private.'

'You *should* maybe go, Rachel.' Dale nods at her. 'And let me sort this out.'

She flounces past us, her hair and dressing gown splaying behind her as she marches to the door before slamming it after herself.

'So I take it that *is* the neighbour?' I glare at him. 'The one that made Tamara so suspicious?'

He at least has the grace to look sheepish. 'Yes, but I never meant—'

'You never do.' I drag a chair out from beneath the table and sit with a thud. I can't bear to sit on the same chair that *woman* just vacated.

'Wayne saw you with her last night.'

'I know.' He hangs his head. 'Look, I'm not proud of myself, Ali. I'd had a few to drink and in any case, it was the first time for a while—'

'So it's happened before then with her?' What a stupid question. Of course it has.

'I called a halt to it when we found out about the baby – I swear to you, but then last night, with Tamara not here, I was really pissed off, and one thing led to another, and—'

'Have you got any more pathetic excuses to make for yourself? Sit down, will you. I don't want to look at you in your pants.' What I've just said would be almost funny if the situation wasn't so sad. The bastard has once again cheated on my sister.

Why does she stay with him? Especially after all the misery she watched our mother endure. She put up with our dad's treatment until she eventually snapped in the worst possible way.

Dale slides into the chair opposite me and rests his head in his hands. 'Are you going to tell Tamara?'

26

ALI

'I'm going to have to tell her, Dale. She'd do the same for me. Where is she, anyway? I've just called into the salon and she's not there.'

'To be honest, I've no idea. She wasn't here at all last night, as I've already said. She didn't even come back after work. I assumed she'd be staying at your place.'

'I haven't spoken to her since Thursday. She hasn't returned any of my texts or calls which has got me worried. She's supposed to be babysitting tonight.'

'So *that's* why you're here.' His face lights up. He's no doubt pleased with the opportunity to gain the upper hand in our conversation.

'Partly, but mainly to check in on her.'

'Ah, come on – you only ever ring her when you want something.'

'That's just not true.'

'So what did the girls at the salon say? Do they know where she is?'

'They told me *you'd* taken her away for the weekend. They said you'd put a note through the salon door giving her an address for a cottage while she was busy doing a treatment. Which after what I've just walked in on, is a complete joke.'

'She probably just didn't want them to know her business.' He plucks a sheet of paper from the fruit bowl between us and slides it across the table. 'This is the only note I know anything about.'

I stare at my sister's slanted handwriting. 'This doesn't make any sense. If she was feeling this low about things between the two of you, she'd have picked up the phone. She always comes to me with her problems.'

He shrugs. 'I know I shouldn't have done what I did last night and I'd do anything for you not to tell Tamara.'

'Is that all you can think about? Getting found out? Anyway, it's not just last night, is it?' He really *is* a bastard. Not a violent one like our father was but a bastard nonetheless.

'I know but somehow, I'll make amends. I'll make it up to her for the rest of my life. Please don't tell her.' He clasps his hands together on the table in front of him as though praying. 'We've got the baby to think of now.'

'You weren't thinking of the baby last night, were you?' I can hardly bear to look at him. My poor sister is probably going to end up as a single mum. She'll probably be better off as one – at least she'll know where she stands.

'I don't know what else you want me to say.'

'Her tyres. What about her tyres? Who's done that to them?'

'I don't know what you're talking about?' He looks puzzled.

'Go and have a look.'

He rises from his chair and heads into the utility room. He emerges a few seconds later having thankfully covered his boxers up with a pair of joggers. As he heads out towards the door, I sigh as I cast my gaze around Tamara's beautiful kitchen. This place was supposed to be their new start after how he treated her in their last home. I can't believe he's done it to her again, nor can I believe I dismissed her fears when we were on the phone. No wonder she's taken off without warning. Or without talking to me.

'Bloody hell.' Dale storms back in, gripping his fringe in his fingers as he turns a circle in the kitchen doorway. 'All four of her tyres – who the hell would do that? This is a decent area – things like that don't happen around here.'

'It wouldn't be that trollop from over the road, would it?' I jerk my head in that direction. My mother would laugh at my use of the word – it was one she used frequently when rowing with my father. Why she stayed with him for so long, I'll never be able to imagine. She allowed him to drive her to do what she did to him in the end.

'Rachel? Nah – she wouldn't do something like that.' He shakes his head. 'It's not her style.'

'She looks to me like she could be capable of *anything*.'

'Has Tamara said much to you this week about that man she keeps seeing outside?' He retakes his seat opposite me.

'A bit,' I reply, ashamed to admit to him that I haven't taken her seriously about that either.

'To be honest, I haven't seen anyone out here.' He joins his hands behind his head and stretches. 'Like I kept telling her, it's probably all in her head.'

'He was outside *here* on Thursday night,' I tell him, remembering the angst in Tamara's voice. 'While I was on the phone to her. I tried to tell her he could have been there for *anything*. He might have just been waiting for a lift.'

'It's what the police said the other night as well. The man, if he *is* hanging around her, hasn't actually done anything. And until he does...' His voice fades.

'Maybe he has.' A cold sensation runs through me. 'Who the hell else would do that to her tyres? It's either that tart you're sleeping with, or *him*.'

My eyes fall on a photo of the two of them pinned to the fridge. And to think they're shortly going to become three. I don't want a niece or nephew of mine to grow up around the same misery we had to suffer as kids. 'I'm going to have to tell her what you've done, Dale. She needs to make her own decision as to whether you deserve another chance.'

His gaze follows mine. 'What if I were to tell you it would *never* happen again?'

'I wouldn't believe you. She only lives over there.' I jerk my finger toward the front of the house.

'But I don't want to lose my wife. Or my baby.' He stares down at the table. 'We moved here for a fresh start. Look, I know I've messed up.' He slaps his palm against his forehead. 'I always mess up. I always think the grass is greener on the other side.'

'Your wife needs you the most right now – like she's never needed you before. I can't believe what you're doing to her.'

'I know.' He brings his hands to rest on the table again. 'It's just, she's been so miserable, so needy and insecure.'

'So sick with the pregnancy hormones,' I add. 'So tired of being on her own all the time. Come on Dale. She deserves so much better.'

'Look, Ali, what if I said, I'll get some counselling. There must be something wrong with me to keep putting my marriage and our future as a family on the line like this. Especially when I love her.'

'Do you?' I stare at him. 'Did you even buy her a card yesterday? Or send her a message to say Happy Valentine's Day? Did you?'

'She knows I think it's all a load of rubbish,' he replies.

'So does Wayne.' A vision of my lovely husband's face enters my mind. 'But he still buys me a card and some flowers. That's what you do when you love someone.'

'I'll make it up to her. And if you let me have this chance, I'll never stop making it up to her.' His expression is so earnest I could almost believe him. Almost.

'Look, I'll have to think about it. And if I *do* decide not to tell her, it'll be for hers and the baby's sake, not yours. But first, we need to find out where she's gone.'

'I know we do.' He pulls a face. 'I honestly thought she'd be with you, especially since she's supposed to be looking after your kids tonight.'

'I've got a really bad feeling about this.' The photo on the fridge and Tamara's smile again catches my eye. 'I've had it since last night when she didn't reply to my texts. Call it sister's intuition, but I know something's wrong.'

'How do you mean?'

'Firstly, if she couldn't look after my kids tonight because she's *gone away*' – I draw air quotes around these words. – 'She'd have been on the phone letting me know.'

'She must be planning to get in touch with you today.'

I shake my head. 'It's even more unusual that she's not even responded to any of my calls or texts. How many times have you tried?'

'Erm, well...'

'Have *you* even *tried* contacting her at all since you arrived home to that note?'

He hangs his head, which tells me everything I need to know. 'What's mostly concerning me now are her tyres,' he says.

'I agree.' I'll ignore that he's changing the subject. 'It's the fact that *all four* of them have been cut. But then there's this *note* the girls at the salon are saying she received. We need to find out where she went in the taxi.'

27

RACHEL

I STORM AROUND MY HOUSE, not knowing what to do for the best. All the time that bitch's car is still parked outside Dale's house. If it wasn't for *her* waltzing in, I could have had the entire weekend with him, totally uninterrupted.

'Bitch,' I scream into the silence.

I'm sick of being on my own. Sick of watching all the happy couples on this street have something that's eluded me for my entire adult life. The only men who *ever* show me any interest are the ones who already *belong* to other women.

I've got so much in common with Dale. We both love the gym, we like the same food, we laugh at similar jokes and there can be no denying the strong attraction between us. Every time, he looks at me, it's with such intensity I feel like the only woman in the world.

The chance of me having children has already passed. And I wanted them, just not to bring up on my own. I can still have marriage though, I can still *live* with someone. I don't want to grow old on my own, yet every time I meet a man who's perfect for me, it turns out he's already spoken for. Sometimes I know from the start, at other times, it doesn't come out straightaway, usually when I'm already invested. This was the case with Dale. I met him at my gym last spring.

'Go on, you can have it.' He gestured at the only available bike in the spin class as we arrived at the same time.

'Oh, I couldn't,' I'd replied. 'At least not without buying you a coffee to say thanks after the class.'

'I'll be in the gym.' He winked at me before leaving the studio.

Our coffees together turned into a weekly occurrence and then an almost nightly one.

I hurried out of work each day, having booked onto the same classes which I knew he enjoyed. Monday was body pump, Tuesday was circuit training. Wednesday was a swim, my favourite as not only could I check him out in his trunks, but we also got time together in the jacuzzi and steam room. Thursday was a HIIT class and Friday was spin. Coffee afterwards became a drink in the bar and chatting became flirting.

Within a month, Dale was the only man in my life, and our gym night get-togethers often turned into hot sex in one of our cars. The best night was when we checked into a hotel, but he'd already gone when I woke up in the morning. And then I didn't see him for a week and had no way of contacting him. The receptionist at the gym wouldn't give out his surname or telephone number and any online searches were fruitless without his full name. I kept telling myself, *he might just be ill.*

I was beyond relieved when he reappeared at body pump the following Monday. It was then that I got a flash of his wedding ring as he picked up his barbell. He'd never worn it before. It's one of the first things I look at in a man – not that it would have ever stopped me from going after him.

I couldn't keep how gutted I was out of my voice as we were

sitting in the bar afterwards. 'You never told me you were married.'

'Yeah, well.' He twizzled his ring around on his finger. 'Things are complicated.'

'Meaning?' It was bad enough that I'd discovered he was married but now I was about to hear chapter and verse about all their problems.

'She's just had a miscarriage,' he replied, avoiding my eye. 'For the seventh time.'

It was bad enough that he was married, but they were obviously trying for a *baby* as well. This meant they were still... I tried to shake that thought from my mind. I couldn't bear to think of the man I'd fallen for with someone else.

'This,' – he pointed from him to me, – 'has to stop. She's not on to me yet, but I can't risk her finding out again.'

'Again?' My voice was a squeak, causing other people in the bar to turn and stare. Of course. Married men don't generally have just one affair. Leopards, spots and all that.

'Yeah, it's happened before,' he admitted. 'The last time was with someone I worked with at my former company. My wife forced me to change jobs, but that wasn't enough. I took the woman I was seeing into our home when Tamara wasn't there, so she's also forcing a house move on me. We agreed that I'd move jobs first and then houses.'

'Tamara, eh?' I didn't like his use of her name. Jealousy crawled up the back of my neck.

'Yeah, it's all been such a mess. I never meant to hurt her, then, or now. I don't want to hurt you either. It's just – well, I'm a man. Us men are easily flattered.'

'I just can't understand why you've never mentioned your wife to me before.'

I thought Dale was different and had hoped we were going places. I also thought he was single. As always, I was wrong.

'Because I enjoy my time with *you.*' He reached across the table and cupped his hand over mine, sending electric shocks up my arm. I knew right then how badly I wanted to win him for myself and the fact that he'd already had more than one affair suggested this wouldn't be the end of things between us. 'When we're together I like to be in the moment, with you, and not thinking about anything or anyone else. You're a good friend, Rachel.'

'Erm thanks.' But the last thing I wanted was to be friend-zoned. I wasn't going to give up on him.

Night after night we continued to meet at the gym and he didn't mention his wife for a while. I certainly wasn't going to bring her into the conversation and cut into our time together. But one evening as Dale picked up his glass, I noticed he was no longer wearing his wedding ring. Hope rose in my belly like champagne bubbles.

'I lost it,' he explained when I asked him. 'We had a day out to the lakes, and it must have slipped off while I was swimming in the water – when my fingers were cold. As you might imagine, Tamara's gone nuts.'

I wasn't interested in anything to do with his bloody wife or what she might have felt like. All I could focus on was that they were out together for the day when he should have been out with *me.*

'Anyway, I won't be here for the rest of the week,' he continued as he pulled a sorrowful face. 'We've got some house viewings lined up after work.'

'House viewings?' Great. They were still planning to move house together. There was a future for them after all.

'Yeah, it was part of her deal for us not to separate after she found out about the woman at work – I think I've mentioned it before. I had to agree to move house. She reckons ours is, you know, tainted.'

I didn't want to think about yet another woman Dale had

slept with. That he was married was bad enough. 'You don't sound too enthused about moving.'

'There's nothing wrong with the house we've got. But she says if we're to have one last go at IVF, she wants to be settled somewhere new and out of the house that—'

'OK, too much information.' I put on my most bored voice. It was the same old, same old every time I met a man. However, I *could* tip the scales of his house move in my favour. I wanted him and his marriage sounded shaky enough for me to get him.

'There's a house right opposite me which has only just gone on the market,' I told him. Not that I'd want *her* around but to have Dale living straight over the road would be pretty amazing. It would only be a matter of time before I'd lure him away from her.

'Really?' A light appeared to come on in his eyes. He's got the nicest eyes – probably the feature that attracted me to him in the first place. 'Tell me more.'

'Well, it's a lovely quiet avenue. And I know the previous owners have done a fair bit of work on the house.' I could still visualise the hordes of workmen. 'The garden's been landscaped, and a new kitchen and bathroom have been put in. However, the man has recently been offered a job overseas so they're looking to leave within the next month. In fact, they've only just reduced the price for a quick sale.'

'And where is this too-good-to-be-true house with a reduced price?'

'The South side of Otley.'

'And it's right opposite you? It certainly sounds too good an opportunity not to at least take a look.'

'If we end up being neighbours, we could share lifts to and from the gym if we ever go from home as well as meeting there after work.' As I said this, the thought of his seemingly insecure wife spotting us returning from the gym was incredibly tantalising. I'd be sure to make it happen.

I honestly believed it would change things, having Dale living right opposite. But I've lost track of the number of times I've paraded around my home with the lights on and the blinds wide open, wearing nothing but my underwear – all in the hope of attracting him back to me.

I got sick of hankering after him from a distance, driving myself mad with longing, when aside from the gym and our drinks, he barely registered my existence when at home. He was still friendly and flirty when we were together, away in our weeknight bubble, but until these last few days, he's never really spoken to me in the street. If it wasn't for his bloody wife.

He was leaving me out in the cold whenever she was around. I felt alone and unwanted, forced to spend time on the other side of the road, just watching him, willing and waiting, until the day that things between us might shift again.

Then last night I got my opportunity, and instead of being confined to a car or a hotel room, we had a proper night – in his *bed*. What a result. All because *she* was completely out of the way.

So hopefully, she won't return.

28

ALI

'WILL FIND *my phone* work even if hers has died?' Dale sits up straighter in his chair.

'Have you set that up on Tamara's?' I glance at the phone in my brother-in-law's hands.

'We sorted it ages ago, when we first got them.'

'I see.'

'But I've never used it to actually look for her,' he adds quickly.

'That's because she's never done anything to betray your trust,' I reply. 'Is it set up so she can also track *you* as well?' As his gaze meets mine, I already have my answer. Of course not.

'I turned it off a while ago.' He looks sheepish. 'Look, I know what you must be thinking of me, Ali, but I promise I'm going to be a better husband. If only I can have another chance.' He looks at me with hope in his eyes. 'And I'll be the best Daddy ever,' he adds. 'Surely you don't want her to go through the next twenty years as a single mother?'

'Don't put that responsibility onto me,' I snap. 'You're the one who's hurting her.'

Thank God I broke the mould when I married Wayne. He'd

never cheat on me, I know he wouldn't. And if he did, I'd just leave. There's no way I could forgive him like my sister keeps forgiving Dale. Why won't she learn her lesson? Isn't what happened between our parents enough of a warning to her? Isn't our mother getting sentenced to eighteen years for voluntary manslaughter enough of a deterrent? We were told she'd get less if she'd have at least *tried* to defend herself. But she just pleaded guilty without even offering any sort of defence for what she did to our father.

'Let's have a look then. It should show her last known location even if her phone is off – I'm sure that's how it works.'

I push my chair back and head to the other side of the table to watch over his shoulder as he thumbs through his settings.

'Eh?' He looks at me, puzzled, then back at his phone. 'According to this, the last time her phone registered was in the middle of the Yorkshire Dales. But it can't be – it's all fields and farms.'

'Zoom in.' I point at the screen. 'Look – there – it's saying Poppy Cottage. And she wrote in her note that she was getting away for a few days, didn't she?' My shoulders relax with relief. At least we know where she is and also that it isn't a million miles from here. 'That's where the taxi must have taken her.' However, this still doesn't explain why she hasn't been in touch since yesterday. Nor does it answer any questions about what happened to her tyres.

Dale's face darkens. 'Maybe she isn't there on her own. What was that about her receiving a note?' His lip curls. 'Nah, she wouldn't – she's carrying my baby for God's sake.'

'Don't you *dare* act all high and mighty about what Tamara may or may not be up to. Not after—'

'Alright, alright.' He pushes his chair back with a scrape as he stands from it, holding the palms of his hands towards me in a mock-surrender gesture. 'I've already told you how much I regret what's happened with Rachel. But I can't turn the clock back, can I? Anyway, I'm going to head over to this Poppy Cottage place. It's about forty minutes away. Are you coming?'

'Of course I am.' I also stand from my chair.

'After all, you'll be wanting your babysitter back, won't you?'

'I want to make sure my sister's alright actually. While all you care about is that she isn't shacked up over there with another man.'

'That's not true. Whether you believe it or not, Ali, I do actually love my wife. I just might not have fully realised it until today.'

Much as I'd like to slap the wounded look off his face after what he's done and how he's driven Tamara away, all that matters is getting over to that cottage she's staying at and checking up on her. Dale's sliding his feet into trainers as I snatch my keys back up from the kitchen table.

'I'll drive,' I say.

'I'll just go and check the bedroom quickly.' he begins. 'She might come back before—'

'There's no time for that.' I start towards the door. 'I'll go on my own if you're going to mess about. You'll have time later to wash your disgusting sheets.'

He locks up as I march up the drive to my car. I can't imagine how I'd feel if Wayne did to me what Dale's done to Tamara. It's the cruellest act. If you're not happy with someone, if you want someone else, at least have the decency to end your current relationship first. What he's done, bringing *her* into their marital bed, beggars belief.

I stare back at the woman who's caused all the trouble. She stands, as blatant as the nose on my face, in her window, just gawping at us through the mist. I feel like going over there and thumping her on my sister's behalf.

'She's having a good look, isn't she?' I yank my seatbelt

across myself as Dale slides into the passenger seat. 'Fancy carrying on with a woman who lives straight over the road. What are you going to do now, move house again?'

'I didn't mean for it to happen last night,' he says. 'I'd called a stop to it all weeks ago when we discovered Tamara was pregnant. But then I got drunk and she was, well – there.'

'*You didn't mean for it to happen,*' I parrot, unable to keep the sarcasm from my voice as I type where we're heading into the sat nav. 'Have you heard yourself?'

'She goes to my gym,' he begins as if that explains everything. 'And we've become quite friendly. It was her who told me about the house being on the market.'

'The plot thickens. Does Tamara know she goes to your gym?' I look at him.

He shakes his head.

'So how did you end up in the pub together last night if you'd supposedly called a halt to things? When Wayne saw you?'

'I'd found that note Tamara left and I was fed up and, well, Rachel came over and wanted to come in. I decided we'd be better going out.'

I shake my head as we pull away from the kerb. I can still feel Rachel's gaze boring into the side of my head. My poor sister.

'When we saw Wayne, we ended up going somewhere else and I had far too much to drink and Rachel's just so easy to talk to,' Dale continues.

'It doesn't sound like the only department she's *easy* in. So then you invited her back to your house?'

'It was a huge mistake.' He lowers his voice.

'Your whole marriage sounds like a mistake as far as I can see.'

'Listen, I love my wife and I really want to be a dad,' Dale repeats. 'I'll understand completely if you decide to tell her but

I'm begging you to let me make amends.' His voice wobbles. He probably means what he's saying in this moment but how long will it last? Only until the next time. 'Honestly, I've really seen the light. I know what matters to me now.'

One thing my mother always taught us was never to trust a person who begins a sentence with the word, *honestly*. After all, she learned the hard way. It's one of the few nuggets of advice I took from her before I decided to cut her from my life.

'Like I said before, I'll have to think about it.' I ease the car out of the street onto the main road. Rightly or wrongly, I *am* beginning to soften with him. The more all this sinks in, the less I want to see my sister hurt any more than she has been already. The prospect of watching her crumple when I tell her she was right to be so insecure about Dale again fills me with dread. She's not had an easy time at all, especially over the last year. She's riddled with anxiety, not sleeping well and her self-esteem has been on the floor. Maybe I can wait until after the baby's born, rather than causing her so much upset while she's pregnant. And in the meantime, I can watch my brother-in-law like a hawk.

'So you're considering it?' I sense his eyes on me as I focus on the road. I can't tell you how—'

'I haven't made my mind up yet.' I turn the demisters up full. 'Let's just get to this cottage, shall we?' Whether I tell Tamara or not, I'm still going to make Dale suffer.

29

RACHEL

THE WAY that sister of hers looked at me as she walked into Dale's house was like I was something she'd trodden in.

It's not as if *I've* done anything wrong. I'm not the one who's married with a baby on the way. Nor have I broken any wedding vows.

I hated Tamara from the moment I saw her across the street. After all, she had everything I wanted. Namely Dale. After so many months of us getting closer, every time we parted ways, I knew he was going back to his wife. It was crucifying.

I could have laughed just after they'd moved in when Tamara bounded over to introduce herself like a playful labrador. As if I could have ever pretended to be her *friend.*

'Hi, I'm Tamara.' She held out her hand as she shook her hair behind one shoulder. 'Your new neighbour.'

I kept my hands firmly behind my back and didn't return her handshake. I didn't even tell her my name. 'Yeah, looks like it,' was all I could muster.

She looked shocked, wounded even, but she didn't give up. 'Have you lived around here for long?'

'Nope,' I replied, looking past her at another of our neighbours.

'Hello,' she called out and I waved back.

Even then, Tamara *still* didn't give up. 'You should pop over for a cuppa sometime,' she insisted. 'It would be lovely to have a friend on the street.'

I half nodded, half shrugged as I turned away. As if.

Two weeks later she was back again.

'We're having an open house for drinks on Friday evening if you fancy joining us,' she said, all high and mighty. I hated her use of *we* and *us*. Perhaps it might have been fun to go, to make Dale squirm, but that probably wouldn't help my endgame. It might have turned him off.

'Thanks but I'll be busy,' I replied. What I didn't add was *with your husband*. I made a mental note to try and delay him at the gym for as long as possible.

Come what may, he was in that gym nearly every weekday night – and so was I. He was serious about keeping in shape and hardly anything got in the way of him being there. I, for one, was never going to pass up a chance for us to be checking each other out across the studio. I spent a fortune on new gym clothes and always knew that eventually, I'd wear him down. It was only a matter of time until he'd be back sleeping with me again. Somehow I'd win him from his wife.

Tamara posted a Christmas card through my door and wished me a Happy Christmas as we were returning home at the same time on Christmas Eve. She looked thin and pale and I knew it was because she was pregnant. Dale had told me they were keeping it quiet until she'd gone past the danger stage. All I could do was hope and pray that she wouldn't.

I couldn't bring myself to return her greeting. There she was, planning Christmas Day with the man who by then, I'd fallen in love with. I'd be able to make him a million times happier than *she* ever could but since the news of her pregnancy, he'd really withdrawn from me again. I've never had to play such a long game with a man but I guess I always knew it would pay off in the end.

He's had at least one affair already so their marriage was already on shaky ground. Also, I've never seen a man less inclined to get home to their wife each evening. He seemed to put it off until the last possible minute. Before and after the news of her pregnancy.

'Does she know you have a drink every night after the gym? It's pushing towards eight o'clock most evenings by the time you get home.' I wrapped my fingers around my mug. We were back to coffee and a chat again instead of bars, hotels and sex in our cars.

'She thinks I finish work at six, not five.' A cloud of guilt which I'd never seen before, entered his eyes. Since the news of this latest pregnancy, he'd changed. And I didn't like it. 'At least she gets the house to herself for a while when she first gets in from her own job.'

'She doesn't have a clue how close *we've* been though, does she? She still keeps trying to get to know me.'

'Of course not.' He sipped his tea. 'She'd have me under lock and key if she knew how much I value your friendship.'

There it was again. That bloody word. *Friendship.* I tried not to flinch as he said it.

'Is that why you only ever give me curt nods across the street if you're leaving the house with *her*.'

He gave me a funny look. No doubt because of my tone when I said *her*. But what did he expect?

'Hey, Rach, I love what we've got. You're fab, you know. And if things were different...' His words faded out but they hung in the air. For weeks I'd waited for him to come back to me. The spark between us was intensifying. If only *Tamara* didn't exist.

'Do you think you'll stay together? From everything I've heard, babies are more of a division than a sticking plaster for relationships.'

He sighed. 'She needs me, do you know what I mean?'

'Not really.'

'I guess we're comfortable, Tamara and me. And then, obviously, we're going to be parents.'

'Shit's comfortable,' I replied. 'But at the end of the day, it's still shit.'

'Things aren't that bad.' He shook his head. 'They've just gotten, like I said, *comfortable*. But I really do enjoy *your* company and I don't want to lose this.' He gestured to me as he looked around us. 'I don't want to lose what *we've* got.'

That warmed me. And as the weeks of this new year have passed, our coffee area at the gym has become one of my favourite places. I live to leave work and head to the gym each evening. To be with him, somewhere that's ours. Somewhere to which Tamara has no access. Other gymgoers must think Dale and I are a couple.

And it's only a matter of time until we are. Properly.

30

TAMARA

I DON'T KNOW how long I've been asleep. What I do know is that I can hardly move. I shuffle amid the sacks I've wrapped around myself and try to shout again but my voice has been reduced to a husk. I'm losing my energy, I'm losing my fight.

I glance around the cellar as if a sudden means of escape will suddenly materialise. Daylight has brought chinks of light through the tops of the walls and I've already gone around several times, pressing on every brick and prodding every nook and cranny trying to find something that's loose. The door at the top of the steps is solid, plus it opens towards me. Until either Martin lets me out, or someone finds me, I'm well and truly trapped.

All seems to have gone quiet in the house above. Either Martin's sitting very still or he's left me alone here to rot. I turn my watch towards my face before I remember it's dead. As I will be if I don't get out of here.

Although I don't know the time, it feels like I've been down here forever. Every minute feels like an hour. I'm starving after not having eaten since the sandwich Sian brought me for lunch yesterday. Unless I count the couple of mouthfuls of steak and peas I tried to get down my neck last night.

My biggest problem is needing a drink. The bastard hasn't even brought any water down – to say last night that he was proclaiming to love me, I could be dead in a heap down here for all he cares. I've been reduced to peeing in a corner and am so cold, my body's devoid of all sensation. I keep thinking about my mother, who also spent her final hours incarcerated. But at least she had light, heat and a little more dignity than I've been afforded.

Mercifully, however, he hasn't raped me. Or worse. Yet. Though the man's capable of anything as he's already told me. My only hope is that Ali will be looking for me by now. She'll have rung or texted me yesterday – I'm convinced of it, especially since I'm supposed to be babysitting tonight. She'll be concerned when I don't reply. As for Dale, he won't give a toss. I bet he's gone to the gym as he often does on a Saturday morning. That's if he's even alone. He's probably invited that slapper from over the road for a drink in my absence. I can just imagine his train of thought. *While the cat's away, the mouse will play.* And I know from bitter experience the games he likes.

I drag myself back to my feet and up the concrete stairs again.

'Martin,' I shout for what must be the thousandth time since he locked me in. 'Please, please, let me out. I'm so cold. Please don't do this to me anymore.' I start to cry again. 'Please, Martin.' I thump at the door. 'Please.' How many times can a person use the word *please*? I can't believe what he's reduced me to. The tears warm my skin, the only warmth I've known since last night. I'm surprised I've got any tears left.

I've known so much misery in the past, with all that happened between my parents, and then Dale's first affair when we'd been married for around eight years. Then he did it to me again last year with his colleague. However, nothing comes close to the misery I'm feeling now. I'm not usually one to feel this hopeless but what hope can a person have when wrapped in sacks in a freezing cellar, surrounded by the stench of one's own urine? No matter how much shouting and running on the spot I continue to do, I don't know how long I can survive without food and water. And even if I do, what effect is this going to have on the baby?

Please Ali. I'm in trouble. Perhaps I can somehow telepathically communicate with my sister. *I'm here. I'm still alive but I might not be for much longer if you don't start looking for me.* I head back down the steps. I'm wasting my breath with my pleas for him to let me out.

I slide down the wall into my corner and pull one of the sacks around my shoulders with a shiver. Why is he doing this to me? I close my eyes. But every time I do, I wonder if it's for the final time.

I blink them open. My baby deserves a chance. And I'm too young to die – I've barely lived yet. After growing up in the shadow of my parent's marriage and all that resulted from that, I've yet to experience what true happiness feels like. I want to feel my baby's fingers curl around mine, I haven't seen much of the world, and I haven't had the chance to expand my business yet. I desperately want to meet my baby and there are so many other things I want to see and achieve. I can't die here. Not at his hands. I've got to keep fighting.

As I struggle to get to my feet, a distant humming is cutting into the silence. Maybe I'm becoming delirious and hearing things now. I try to quieten my breath.

I can *definitely* hear a humming. Oh my God, it could be a car. It's becoming louder and louder. Perhaps someone's coming this way. Maybe I'm going to be rescued at last. I hold my breath. Yes – it's a car, alright. It could be Dale – it could *really* be Dale.

31

TAMARA

I RUSH TO THE STEPS. The car sounds like it's come to a halt right outside. The still-running engine is the most welcome noise I've ever heard. But what will be even better is the sound of slamming doors signalling that someone's getting out of the car. I just pray I can make myself heard to whoever it is.

Two doors slam. I'm going to get out of here. I'm really going to get out of here. Ali must have looked for me at the salon. One of the girls might have remembered the place I was going which was written on the note. Or they might have got in touch with Uber.

I can hear muffled words but being below-ground, I can't make out what's been said, especially of the person who's replying. I'm only catching the odd note of the deeper voice. But I'm certain it's Dale's.

'Help!' I find my footing on the stairs. 'Please help me.' I try to shout but my voice isn't any stronger than the last time I tried. Somehow, I've *got* to make myself heard. This could be my only chance of getting out of here.

I might have seriously underestimated my husband. He could have been up all night looking for me, tearing his hair out when I didn't respond to my phone. And now he's here to rescue me.

'Dale,' I try to call out again. 'Ali.' I can't think who else might be with him. I'm only halfway up the steps when the door at the top of the cellar bursts open and bangs against the wall. As the footsteps pound the concrete and I see the shape of the person, I know I could be done for.

'Keep quiet,' Martin hisses as he descends the steps. 'Do you hear me?'

I turn to rush back down before he can sweep me along in his path. Just before he reaches me at the bottom, I trip backwards, landing in the sack pile but cracking my head on the wall behind. For a few moments, darkness swims around me. Lights flash behind my eyes and I'm sure I can still hear voices. But they sound like they're far away.

Am I dead? Or have I knocked myself out?

I come to as Martin drops to his knees beside me and squeezes his hand over my mouth. I'm still very much here but my head's in agony from where I've hit it. 'Help,' I try to shout again, but then taste the sweat on his palm as he presses down harder. 'If you stay quiet, I won't hurt you,' he says.

I squeak and squeal as I try to hook my fingers beneath his palm. At least his hand's only across my mouth. It's no good – he's too strong for me. But if I can calm myself, if I can try to breathe through my nose, I can survive this. However, if I continue to struggle and keep trying to cry out, he's going to kill me, of that I'm certain.

'Tamara.' It *is* my husband's voice. 'Are you in there?' He's banging at the front door and repeatedly ringing the doorbell.

'Tamara.' Ali's here too, just as I thought. It sounds as though she's shouting through the letter box. 'It's me, Ali. Look, I know you've been upset but please just let me in. Dale doesn't have to come in with me, not if you don't want him to.' The sound of her voice brings tears to my eyes as I continue to snort air through my nose. Martin's grip doesn't tighten but it doesn't relax either. 'Just keep still and quiet and everything will be OK,' he hisses. I feel too dizzy to move anyway. I wouldn't be surprised if I've got a concussion after the second smack I've taken to the head.

'Come on, sis, open up – I know you're in here. Your phone says so.'

My phone. Of course. It'll have shown up on our *Find My Phone* app. I forgot about that but thank God. At least they won't give up on me now. Surely they'll keep trying until they find a way in, even if that means getting the police to break the door down.

I've just got to hang in here. Help's coming. Martin *must* realise this.

'Tamara.' The letterbox rattles again. She isn't giving up. 'I just need to know if you're alright. Just tell me that, then if you want to be alone, if you want me to go away again, I'll respect that.' Dale must have shown Ali the note I left in the kitchen.

Tears leak from my eyes into my ears as Martin continues to press his hand across my mouth. But I firmly believe it's just to silence me. If he was going to choke me to death, he'd have done it by now.

The hammering continues around the other windows.

Please, please I silently pray. *Please let them be able to somehow get in here.* But I already know they won't. This cottage is as solid as a fortress, the windows and doors are locked and the windowpanes are too small to facilitate any kind of entry or exit. I'd have been through one of them last night if that had been an option.

I let out another whimper.

'Shut up, I said.' Martin's voice is a low snarl. But he loosens his grip enough for me to be able to move my jaw for a second and sink my teeth into his skin.

'Arrgh.' He pulls his hand away and I try to roll to the side to destabilise him, but he clamps me between his legs and brings both hands over my face this time. 'One more sound out of you and I'll just leave you down here, do you hear me?'

'Tamara.' Dale's shouting into the letter box now. 'Sweetheart. Just open up, will you? We need to know that you and the baby are OK.'

Sweetheart. He never calls me that. What I wouldn't give to see his face. And my sister's face. I just pray they don't give up.

32

ALI

'MAYBE SHE'S GONE for a walk or something.' Dale points through the mist at the hills behind the cottage. 'It's not a million miles from the reservoir here, is it?'

'Without opening any of the curtains?' I nod back at the cottage. 'No, she's a stickler for letting the daylight in.' I think back to when we used to share a bedroom. 'I don't know what it is but I have a really strong sense that she's in there, hiding from us.'

'She'd have come to the door if she was inside.' Dale continues to stare at the house. 'Especially when she heard *your* voice.'

'What if she *can't* get to the door?' A vision of the slashed tyres slams into my brain and is swiftly followed by another image, one that I attempt to blink away. 'What if she's hurt?'

'I honestly don't think she's here.' Dale shakes his head.

'But the app on your phone said she was.'

'Maybe she *was* last night but perhaps she's moved on. I still think the most likely explanation is that she's gone for a walk.'

'I guess her being *here* would explain why she's not been

answering her calls and texts,' I say. 'Look.' I thrust my phone screen at him. 'Mine has no service. Has yours?'

'Mine's the same.' He pulls his phone from the pocket of his joggers and the face of my sister smiles out from it. Something in what he was saying before must be true. If he has a photograph of her as his phone's wallpaper then he must love her more than I'm giving him credit for. So why sleep with another woman? He's clearly concerned about Tamara so why has he risked his marriage and his chances of a family? Anyway, I can't focus on that right now – all that matters is finding her. 'I have no service either – I reckon the fog will have weakened any hope of getting a signal even more than usual.'

'OK, so I'll go with your theory about her going for a walk.' I glance around for a public footpath sign. 'After all, she's got no reason to ignore *me* at the door. I guess I'll have to accept she's not here.' I sigh as I glance back at the car. 'So what now? Should we just wait here for her to come back?'

'We could have a drive around – she can't have gone far, can she?'

'Good idea.' I'm glad he's not thinking of giving up on her. I just want to see her face and know that she's safe, even if she'd prefer to be left alone this weekend. But it's a relief to slide back into the driver seat of my BMW and be back in the warmth. It's so chilly out there and in my haste to look for Tamara, I didn't even grab a coat on my way out of the house.

Dale returns to his seat so I start the car up again.

'I hope she's wrapped up warm if she's gone out walking,' I say with a shiver.

'I don't like the idea of her walking alone out here. Especially in this fog.' The seatbelt warning beeps, so he drags the seatbelt across himself. 'Not to mention that she's three months pregnant and there's no phone signal whatsoever.'

I navigate the sharp bend away from the cottage and then

glance at him. He's seriously rattled at being unable to find her. No doubt it will intensify his guilt after what he did last night. And not only last night. Good. He deserves to feel shitty.

'Turn left here.' He points to another single-track road. We've already gone at least half a mile. 'I'm pretty sure this road leads towards the reservoir.'

My phone is lit up in the dashboard cradle but Google Maps is still saying *no service*. At least we're doing *something*. However, if there's no sign of her as we drive around, I'm not too sure what we'll do next.

'It's just one straight road,' I say after a few minutes. 'We're getting further and further away from the cottage. Surely she won't have walked this far.'

'Stop.' He points at a Ford S-Max that looks like it's been abandoned in a hedge. 'What the hell's *that* doing there?'

I pull up in a passing place just after it and without speaking, we simultaneously unclip our seatbelts, slam our doors and rush towards the car. My heart's in my mouth as I contemplate whether its occupants could have been dead all night in there. What the hell are we about to see? I steel myself.

'What if it's Tamara?' My voice is so small it's barely perceptible.

'That's just gone through my head as well.' All colour has drained from Dale's face. 'I really don't like how close it is to where her phone last registered.'

'You go first.' As we reach the rear of the car, I hang back to allow Dale to go first. This could be the moment everything changes. The moment when I lose my sister and unborn niece or nephew forever. Aside from Wayne and my boys, she's my only family – I can't lose her. I hold my breath as Dale reaches the driver's door and tries it.

'It's locked and there's no one inside.' He lets a long breath out.

'Thank God.'

He squeezes himself into the hedge and around the bonnet. 'Nor is there any sign of damage.'

'How odd.' I cup my hands against one of the back windows as I peer inside. There's nothing to suggest anything sinister has happened. A couple of reusable Asda bags and a discarded Costa cup. I glance back to the road. There are no tyre marks leading from it. What a strange place to abandon a car.

'It must be stolen,' Dale says. 'Take a photo, just in case.'

As I pluck my phone from my bag and open it up, the roar of another car emerges from nowhere as it whizzes along the single track behind us. 'What the—' I spin around but it's already disappeared into the mist.

'Someone's in a rush,' Dale remarks as he looks up from peering into the passenger side. 'But I can think of better roads to crash on than the ones around here.'

'That's the only car I've seen since we left the main road down from Otley,' I reply. 'Yeah, you'd be in trouble crashing out here if there's only one car an hour to find you.'

'If *that*,' Dale replies.

'Do you think we should report this? Is that why I'm taking a photo?'

'Yeah, when we find a signal. There must be at least a bit around here for Tamara's phone to have shown up on that app.'

'You don't think this car is linked to her in any way, do you? After all, we know she's not in her own car.'

'Nah.' He scrambles out of the hedge. 'But the owner of this one's probably looking for it.'

Not that we can report *anything* yet. Not until we find a signal. And find a signal we must – just in case my sister's been trying to get hold of me since we've been out of range.

'Do you think she's OK, Dale? I can't stop thinking about those tyres, and that stalker.'

'Of course she is.' He rests his hand on my arm. 'She's just trying to teach me a lesson. She's done it before, after all.'

'That doesn't explain her not responding to *me*, though, does it?' I start back towards my car. 'When I ring this in, I'm going to mention her going missing to the police as well.'

I've got a really bad feeling and as the minutes tick by, it's only intensifying.

33

RACHEL

I TOOK a massive risk putting my foot down on that road but I had to get past them without being seen. I've no idea how they could have known to look around here. *Nobody* knows where this place is. I remember when I took it over after my aunt's death earlier this year and had to arrange a clearance firm and a multitude of deliveries to transform it into something that could be listed on AirBnB. Sat nav would always get the deliveries here but when they were trying to reprogramme them to find their way out again, there was never any signal.

I haven't rented the place out to anyone yet, so I can only hope it has a far-reaching appeal if and when I do. It's cosy, secluded and set in picturesque surroundings. It should have been perfect for this weekend's purpose but instead, it's turning into something I hadn't reckoned on.

As I get onto the final run towards the cottage, my mind drifts back to the last time I beckoned Martin into my house a week or so ago.

'Get in here now,' I hissed into the darkness, praying no one had seen him. If Tamara had returned to her window right at that moment, my carefully thought-out plan would come to nothing. No way could she find out that Martin and I had struck up an allegiance in the preceding few weeks. I hadn't invited him in *every* time I'd noticed him hanging around, but often enough to persuade him I was on his side.

'She doesn't even have a clue I exist,' he complained as he wrapped his fingers around a hot mug. 'And I don't know how to change things.'

'That's where you're wrong,' I replied. 'How could she *not* know? You're out on that street often enough.'

'I'd treat her a million times better than *he* does,' he went on, ironically echoing the sentiment I harboured towards Dale where Tamara was concerned. 'She looks so thin and miserable, and they always seem to be arguing from what I've seen and heard.'

'She's just waiting, you know.' I pulled the blind down.

His head jerked up from where he'd been staring into his tea. 'Waiting for *what*?'

'For you to make a move of course.' I sank into the chair facing him. 'She's not the type of person to make the first approach – she told me that herself. So if you're interested in her, it's all down to you.'

'You're *friends* with Tamara?' He jerked his head in the direction of her house. 'You didn't tell me that the last time we were talking.'

'Didn't I? Well, of course we're friends – she only lives across the road.'

'What exactly has she said to you?' He sat up straighter in the armchair.

'Well, as you already seem to know, her marriage is hanging by a thread.'

His face lit up as he studied me intently, waiting for me to bestow my next crumb of hope. As long as I kept my relation-ship with Dale completely out of what I was telling him, as well as news of the wretched *baby*, I had no doubt I could pull it off.

'Anyway, she *has* noticed you and wonders why you never talk to her if you like her.'

'Really?' He spluttered on a mouthful of tea. I watched as beige droplets flecked the arm of my lovely white armchair. It took all I had not to react and order him back out onto the street but somehow, I managed it.

'She reckons you,' – I pointed at him, – 'could be the one to rescue her from her miserable existence. They say everyone has a fantasy.' I laughed then, enjoying setting them up even more than I thought I would.

'You're joking, aren't you?' He sat up straighter in his seat and I could tell from his face he was buying what I was telling him. I'd given him no reason not to. 'She really said *that*?'

'She also thinks you're just her type.' I allowed my face to relax into a smile. 'And don't get too big-headed here but what was the exact word she used?' I pretended to think for a moment. 'Oh yes, *gorgeous*. She thinks you're gorgeous, Martin.'

He flushed to the roots of his hair. So far, my plan was work-ing. He really believed me. 'Oh my God, so what shall I do now?'

'I reckon she'd respond well to a grand gesture,' I said. 'And it's Valentine's Day in a few days.'

'I know.' His smile faded. 'I *could* send her flowers or some-thing but that won't exactly bring us together, will it?'

'No, but you could *invite* her somewhere,' I said. 'To a place you could be completely alone.'

'Like my house?' he asked. 'I can't imagine she'd accept that. She doesn't even know me.'

'No, I'm thinking of somewhere that's on more neutral ground,' I replied. 'Somewhere that could have been booked especially as a Valentine's Day treat.'

'That's all well and good but how would I persuade her to come?' He looked crestfallen. 'After all, she's still technically married.'

'What if I told you I had a perfect plan for *all* of it,' I replied. 'And that you could keep her with you for as long as you want to.'

'I'd keep her there forever,' he said. 'Oh my God, you don't know how long I've waited for things to change like this.'

I reached forward, resting my hand on his arm. 'Sometimes in life, you just have to go after what truly matters – with everything you've got. Rather than waiting for it to come to you.'

I was speaking for myself more than for Martin.

The rest of the plan went like clockwork. Getting Tamara to my aunt's cottage couldn't have gone any smoother. She fell for it harder than a storm of hailstones. She was out of my way *far* easier than I could have ever anticipated.

The only fly in the ointment was Dale. He messaged yesterday afternoon to say he was giving the gym a miss, so I did too. However, I was gutted to arrive home to find him having taken what must have been an early finish and be walking up their drive with a bouquet of flowers. Meant for *her*.

Thankfully, he walked straight past the Fiat's tyres, which I'd slashed in the early hours with a Stanley knife. It's the first time I've done anything like it but I needed to ensure she couldn't just jump in her car and drive back. I wanted her to be forced to take a taxi to her weekend abode, and with the lack of signal, to struggle to get a return journey. Well, I say weekend, really I wanted her to *never* come back.

It was nearly seven when dressed to the nines, I rang Dale's doorbell. He answered with a glum look on his face and a glass of what looked like whiskey in his hand.

'What on earth's up with you?' I stepped over the threshold

without being invited. 'You've cancelled our gym session and our Friday drinks, and for *what*? To sit around in your joggers, drinking on your own.' I pointed at his glass.

'Tamara's gone off for a few days.'

'Gone? Really?' I followed him into the kitchen. It had all worked – it had bloody worked.

'She left me a note saying she needs space to get her head around things. She's not happy and I don't really blame her.'

It couldn't have gone any better. Tamara's note hadn't even factored into my original plan so when he showed me it, I could hardly stop my face from breaking into an excited grin. It felt like fate then. Dale and I were clearly more meant to be than I'd ever imagined.

'To be honest, everything's changed since she got through her twelve-week scan,' he said, his expression a cross between anguish and guilt. 'I want a family, Rach. I don't want a kid of mine growing up without me.'

This was where my plan was *not* going as intended. 'Let's go out,' I said, catching hold of his arm. 'I'll cheer you up.' I was sick of hearing about this *baby* that would be barely bigger than a walnut. There could be no denying that Dale had changed considerably towards me since finding out. And I was so right to bring Martin into things at this point. I hadn't realised she'd reached the twelve-week stage already. This meant the shit was getting more real so there is even more urgency to ensure she and Dale are wrenched apart.

Dale doesn't truly want Tamara. He just wants to be a dad, which at my age, is something I can't offer him. But I can still get in between them.

'And how are you going to propose to cheer me up?' he replied with a wry smile as he leaned against the counter. Good, something of the old Dale was back. The Dale who'd existed before the wretched pregnancy.

'Like I always do. Come on. Put your glass down and let's get out of here.'

'But I'm over the limit.' He drained his glass and set it down.

'We'll get a cab. I've had a glass of wine as well.'

'What if she comes back while I'm out?'

'Judging by what I've just read, I wouldn't hold your breath.' I knew there wasn't the remotest chance of her coming back. I also knew that by the end of the night, I would have Dale exactly where I wanted him. In *her* bed.

I'm queasy with nerves at what's to come. The only way he's going to move forward with me is to get her out of the picture. Permanently. I love Dale, I can't get away from that. And I'll do whatever it takes to keep him. And the knowledge I gained from befriending Martin should help with that.

At least Dale and that bloody sister were a couple of miles away from the cottage when I saw them. Dale's car was pointing away from here so it looks like they've already been and gone.

Which gives me plenty of time to instigate part two of the plan.

34

TAMARA

'It wasn't supposed to be like this.' In the chink of light from the top of the cellar steps, I watch Martin's outline as he paces from one edge of the cellar to the other.

'How *was* it supposed to be then? You've tricked me into coming to this place, pissed all over me, locked me down here—'

'None of that would have happened if you'd just treated me like you were supposed to.'

'I'm not some puppet, Martin,' I reply. 'I have thoughts and feelings of my own.'

'But I don't know what to do *now* – that's the problem. If *they've* been here already, they're bound to come back.'

'We could go somewhere else,' I tell him. 'You've got a place in Skipton, right?' If I can get him to agree to this, as soon as we've driven into civilisation, I can attract attention to summon some help.

'Like I can *really* trust *you*. You tried to bite me just now.'

'To get your hand off my face.' I stamp my foot which I'm starting to feel again thanks to my recent exertions creating some fresh blood flow. 'You've locked me in here like an animal. Wouldn't *you* do anything to get out?'

He pauses his pacing and swings around to face me. 'You're right. And I promise I'll make it up to you.'

I could drop to the floor in relief. He's going the other way again. It's as though he's blocked the baby from his mind. Either that or he's accepted it.

'Just let me out of here. Please let me get warm.'

'You've got to believe me when I say I *never* wanted any of this – I only wanted *you*.'

'And you've got me.' I put everything I can into softening my voice. I might not be able to get out of this house immediately, but him letting me out of this cellar is a start. I don't know where Dale and Ali have gone but when they come back, which I'm sure they will, I'll be able to make myself heard if I'm up there rather than in the cellar. 'Look, I'm sorry things went so sour – let's try again, shall we?'

'But what about *that*?' He points at my stomach and I grimace at my precious baby being referred to as a *that*. Especially after everything I've gone through to get to this stage.

'I don't have all the answers. But we'll work it out.' I rest my hand on my belly, praying the baby is still safe after all the stress I've been under and the two falls I've endured. I keep telling myself that it's snug in its sack of amniotic fluid and tougher than I give it credit for.

'How do I know I can trust you?' Oh shit. He's not moving to allow me to head back up the steps. He can't change his mind now, he just can't.

'How can we *ever* know whether someone can be trusted?' Dale's face enters my mind as I'm struck by the irony of my words. It's followed by my father's, and I scrunch my eyes closed to rid myself of it. I've been seeing his face more and more lately which can never be a good thing. 'Look, what's the alternative here, Martin?' Hopefully, my use of his name will soften him. 'You're not the type of man who'd leave a woman down here to freeze or starve to death.'

'Why do you have to bring up what type of man I am?' His voice is full of anguish. 'I should never have told you anything.'

'All I meant was that it's been hard enough for you to live with what happened with your wife each day. If you kill *me*, how will you manage to live with yourself then? You told me you loved me.'

'And I loved Belinda.' His voice rises. 'What happened was never meant to. And neither was any of *this*. You were supposed to sleep in bed with *me* last night. We were going to be happy. We—'

'And we still can be happy.' I step towards him and grip each of his arms. He's so close to letting me out of here – I've got to keep appeasing him. 'Please, Martin – why don't you make us some tea and toast while I go upstairs and get myself cleaned up? I'm so hungry and so cold.'

He flinches. 'I don't know if that's a good idea. What if—'

'It'll all be fine – I promise.' I let go of his arms. 'Just let me have a change of clothes from the bag I brought with me and then we can sit down and work out what to do from here.' It's an effort to keep my voice light and airy. I'm so stressed and exhausted, I really don't know how I'm holding it all together. 'What do you think?'

He shuffles from foot to foot. I'm certain that I'm wearing him down.

'I've really learned my lesson, Martin – I'm not going to try anything stupid, honestly.' I don't take my eyes off his face. 'I'm not going to risk being locked down here again, am I?'

'I *have* been lonely up there,' he admits. 'Last night certainly wasn't the night I'd intended for us. And I'd have let you out sooner, but I was panicking. I didn't know what to do for the best.' The two of us are so close to one another, we're at kissing distance. And for one awful moment, it seems that he might do that.

'There you go then.' I tap his arm as I step back. 'Let's put all this behind us and start again.'

'*If* we go to Skipton,' he says. 'You'll have to travel in the boot.'

'Why?'

'So no one sees you.'

There goes my plan of attracting attention. Perhaps my only opportunity will be when I arrive at his house. But no, of course, he lives in a converted farmhouse which is out on a limb.

The thought of travelling in the same spot as his dead wife fills me with horror; however, I wonder what the chances are of him driving the same car six years on. Surely he wouldn't have kept it.

But I've got to stay positive – at least I'll be alive. And if we end up at his house, there's bound to be more chances to escape. He won't have prepared it for my arrival like he has here – removing keys from window locks and all that. However, I need to play for time and to get him to remain *here* for as long as possible. Eventually, Dale and Ali will come back. They have to.

35

TAMARA

I MIGHT STILL BE TRAPPED in this cottage but I've never been more grateful for a drink of water in my entire life. I scoop it from my hands to my lips directly from the tap as the shower warms up.

As the stench of what I've been through is rinsed down the plughole, I begin to feel slightly more human. I'm not particularly hungry but know I need food. After all, it isn't just myself I've got to look after.

'I'll leave these here for you, darling.'

So he's calling me *darling* now. My flesh creeps not only at his words but at the prospect of him being in such close proximity. The prospect of him seeing me naked isn't a good one. But I had to get showered. I had to free myself from the clothes he's made me wear and the pee he sprayed me with last night.

'I'll leave it a few minutes before I put some tea and toast on for us. Give you a chance to get sorted.'

'Thank you.' I'm praying he doesn't come any closer.

I hold my breath for a few seconds before poking my head

around the shower screen to check he's gone. The leggings and fleecy jumper from my holdall are draped over the towel rail. As well as my own socks and clean underwear. When I get out of here, I'll *never* take this sort of thing for granted again.

Thankfully, he hasn't hung around. I can hear him downstairs, so I know I'm safe to sit on the loo, unwatched. Not like last night. Now that my first scan has confirmed everything's OK, I'm not checking for bleeding quite as often as I was a few weeks ago, but I'm still paranoid. Especially now.

I let a long sigh of relief out. There's no blood but I'm still getting the occasional twinge in my lower abdomen. As soon as I get free from here, I'm going to the hospital. Until I hear the sound of that heartbeat again, there's no way I'll be able to relax.

As I rub my hair with a towel, voices echo from downstairs. Is it the TV or the radio? No, one of them is definitely Martin, but who could the other one be? It can't be Dale or Ali having returned. They'd have been straight up here, looking for me if they'd managed to get in. I tug my jumper over my head and creep to the door. I don't know whether to be hopeful or terrified.

'I want to see her right now,' a female voice insists. 'When I've shown her this little lot, she won't want to go home anyway.'

'She doesn't want to be here either.' Martin's voice is flat. 'And if you'd told me she was pregnant—'

'From what I've heard, she'll probably lose it anyway.'

Who the hell is it?

'You promised she was waiting for me to do something, *a grand gesture*, you said.' Martin's voice veers between sarcasm and anguish as he speaks. 'But things couldn't have gone any more wrong.'

If someone's in the lounge, it means an outside door has been recently opened so I might be able to make a run for it. I creep down the stairs, placing my feet at the edge of each step to minimise the chance of squeaks as I descend. The rose petals have been cleared away, the petals I was so certain had been my husband's doing. I flit to the door, my heart hammering in my chest as I try the handle. Shit – it's locked. I should have known it would be.

'Things might have gone wrong for *you*.' I creep towards the lounge door. The voice is familiar. Catty, yet confident. 'For me, everything went just as planned,' whoever it is continues. 'As our dear Tamara is just about to find out.'

'Find out *what*?' Since there's still no way of getting out of here, I might as well confront this. I stand in the lounge doorway and stare at the petite blonde, wearing jeans and a puffa jacket with her back to me as she faces Martin. Then I gasp as she swings around to face me, her expression smug. Maybe I've been in that cellar too long, and I'm seeing things. But no, it's *her* from over the road. The bitch that's been making a play for my husband. 'What the hell are *you* doing here?'

'It's my house actually.' She stretches her arms out, displaying the flats of her palms as if that denotes her ownership. 'I trust you're enjoying your stay here with Martin.' She smiles, revealing her perfect teeth.

'But– what— I don't understand.' It was only yesterday when she and I had a confrontation in the street. How have we gone from barely knowing each other to her turning up at the cottage where I've been held captive since early yesterday evening? How does she even know where I am? Unless— I stare at her condescending expression. Surely not. *How could they*?

'Did the two of you arrange this?' They must have done. It's the only explanation. How else would she know where I am?

'Let's just say I helped to facilitate your lovely weekend break.' Her face breaks into a broader smile. 'But I was more than happy to play Cupid, especially since it was Valentine's

Day. I trust Martin's been treating you just as you deserve to be treated?'

She's set this up. She's done this to me.

'What the hell are you playing at?'

'I'm not *playing* at anything, Tamara.' The smile vanishes from her face as quickly as it arrived. 'I'd better spell things out to you so we both know where we stand, hadn't I?'

I look from her to Martin. Suddenly, out of the two of them, he seems the less unhinged.

36

ALI

'WELL?' I stand at the bottom of the stairs as I call up to my brother-in-law. 'What's she taken? Can you tell?'

'Not a great deal as far as I can see.' His voice echoes from one of the rooms above. 'Her toothbrush and a few bits from her dressing table, but — a door slams. 'Her passport's still here.'

'She's hardly likely to go running off to another country when she's three months pregnant, is she? Hang on, what's that?' I notice a book poking out from a drawer in her hallway table, saying 'stalker log' on the front. I stride over to it and begin leafing through the pages. She's never mentioned *this* before.

Monday 6 Jan
18:36 A man was peeing against the garage wall. Think it was him, but no one was in the garden by the time I got outside.

What the hell is she doing, going outside on her own to confront a situation like that?

> Tuesday 7 Jan
> 12:21 He's been hanging around outside the salon all morning. Sian went out to approach him, but he ignored her and walked away.

Again, what is she playing at?

> Wednesday 8 Jan
> 17:25 He's driven behind me for the entire journey back from work. Now, he's hanging around outside on the other side of the road.

> Thursday 9 Jan
> 18.07 He followed me right around the supermarket and stared at me from the next aisle as I was paying. I shouted, 'Why are you following me?' But everyone just looked at me like I was mad as he disappeared into the crowd. Maybe I am.

Friday 10 Jan
19:15 I heard footsteps behind me as I was walking to my book club. Every time I stopped and turned, there was no one there, but one of the girls who was late said she'd seen someone hanging around too. He'd gone by the time we all went to check.

Saturday 11 Jan
20:07 He was standing at the bar while I was at the cinema with Lisa and kept looking over at us. We ended up booking a taxi to take us both home as Lisa was too scared to catch the bus.

This is horrendous. There's a diary entry for every single day for several months. I slap my hand against my forehead. To think I didn't take her seriously on the odd occasion when she's mentioned all this. If she'd shown me this book before, I'd have frogmarched her to the police and wouldn't have allowed her to be fobbed off.

Sunday 12 Jan.
11:22 He was on the other side of the football pitch when I was watching Edward at his match. He didn't seem to be watching anyone – apart from me.

To think the man's been in the vicinity of one of my sons is making me feel even worse. I should have listened to my sister. Then she might have felt more able to tell me the full extent. But as usual, I've been too wrapped up in the day-to-day of my own life. Dale was right to a certain extent – the only reason I even rang her on Thursday was to check that she was still available to babysit the boys.

Monday 13 Jan
18:37 He's hanging around outside the house again. He's been there for over an hour. Still, he isn't doing or saying anything. I wish he'd speak, I wish I knew what he's doing and why he keeps coming back.

Tuesday 14 Jan
18:11 He's outside the house again. He doesn't do anything. He just stares. I'm so stressed.

This must have been awful for her. It's a miracle she's made it safely to her twelve-week scan with all this going on.

Wednesday 15 Jan
19:52 He's back outside the house. He disappeared

when Dale was parking up and had vanished completely when I sent Dale back outside to check.

And so it continues. I stare across the street at the spot in which he must have been standing. Mainly, the diary consists of him being outside here every night, but it seems he was pursuing Tamara all over the place. He's followed her to the salon and he's hung around when she's been meeting friends. I'd be surprised if he doesn't know where I live as well. I wonder if she's ever shown this diary to the police. And to think I was trying to put her mind at rest by telling her he was probably waiting for a nightly lift to work or something. No, he's been stalking her. And now she's disappeared.

'We need to call the police.' I snap the book closed and look at my brother-in-law as he arrives at the bottom of the stairs. 'This stalking thing has been even worse than she's let on.'

'I really don't think there's any need to panic.' He takes the book from me and opens it at a random page before skimming top to bottom. 'Looking at these entries, this has all been going on for a while. If the man was going to do something to her, he'd have done it by now.'

'She's carrying your bloody baby!' My voice is a screech which echoes around the hallway. I can hardly believe I'm having to remind him of this. 'You could look at least a *bit* concerned.'

'Alright, alright.' He continues to scan the page. 'I *am* concerned. I had no idea she was keeping this log of things.'

'I didn't either. Nor did I know it was happening this often. We need to make that call *now*.'

37

ALI

DALE LOOKS AROUND, presumably for wherever he put his phone. But his response to this is far too slow for my liking.

'I'll ring them.' I delve into my handbag. I can't trust him to make the police aware of just how serious her disappearance is.

'I'm quite capable of doing it myself.' He frowns. 'Besides, she's *my* wife.'

I quickly read the message Wayne's sent me before swiping it to the side so I can make the call.

> Have you found that errant sister of yours yet? Dad says he'll have the kids. Call me when you can. x

'*Your* wife? Don't make me laugh. Not after who I caught you with this morning.'

'I've already told you how much I regret it all.'

'That's not good enough, Dale.'

'You still haven't said for certain whether you're going to tell her anything.' He cocks his head to one side as he waits for my answer.

'I'm still thinking about that. Look, I don't care what you say,

I'm calling them. Besides I've got the registration plate of that car which we still need to report.'

'But how's *that* going to be related to Tamara?' He lowers his phone.

'Hopefully, it isn't, but it could be.'

'Besides, now I've had the chance to think about it,' he goes on. 'I reckon it's some teenagers who've hijacked their parent's car, then abandoned it in a hedge before running off. They'll be scared of getting caught.'

'Yeah, whatever. But it was too close to that cottage for my liking. The police might as well check both things at the same time.'

I jump as a figure approaches the frosted glass of the door and then jump again when a pile of letters plops onto the door-mat. 'What number should I ring, do you think? The three nines?' As if I'm asking Dale for advice. I honestly don't think he'd be reporting her missing if I hadn't turned up. It's a bloody good job she was supposed to babysit.

'It's hardly an emergency, is it?' He bends down to the post on the mat. 'In fact, as soon as we show them the note she's left behind, they'll tell us she's a grown woman, perfectly entitled to leave on her own accord. I bet they won't even do anything.' He begins leafing through his letters. As though anything in those could be more important than making sure Tamara's safe. 'So just ring 101.'

'We should leave the note out of it for now,' I reply. 'I'm going to tell them about *everything* apart from that.'

He starts to say something but I shush him as I key in 101.

'This is the non-emergency line for the police service. After the tone, please state where you are calling from.'

'Otley, Leeds.' My voice shakes. As if I'm having to do this.

'Connecting you to West Yorkshire Police. Please hold the line.'

'Thank you for calling West Yorkshire Police, you are number two in the call queue.'

Aargh. 'I still think we should have called 999, Dale. What if she's in some sort of trouble?' I still can't shake the feeling that she is. Deep in my bones, I know my sister needs me to find her.

'I really don't think she will be. Honestly, Ali, I reckon she *was* in that cottage and just wants to be left alone. Perhaps you should re-read her note since you're in so much doubt.'

'What you mean is *you* can't face her after what you've done behind her back.' I stride into the lounge which doesn't feel the same without her in it. And I don't want to look at my brother-in-law's guilty face for a moment longer. I'll leave him looking at his letters.

'Yes, hello. I'd like to report a missing person.' I pace the room as I reel off the details, leaving no stone unturned. I tell the operator about the tyres, and how out of character Tamara going off grid like this is. Then I tell him about the car in the hedge and read out the registration. Finally, I tell him about her stalker fears and read him some of the entries from over the past week.

'He's been outside her house every night,' I add as I pull the curtains open. 'I just didn't grasp how scared she was. And I think she *was* inside that cottage when I called there with her husband,' I continue. 'And I've got an awful feeling she's not on her own.'

'We'll send a patrol car within the next two hours,' the operator promises.

'*Two hours*?' My voice rises. 'But what if—'

'This isn't the emergency line you've called, madam.'

'So what if I were to call it now?' I suddenly realise how right Dale was. If I'd mentioned her note, they probably wouldn't be going around there at all. 'Would they get there any faster then?'

'The fact that you've called 101 tells me you don't view this as an emergency either.'

'Well, I do – of course I do. My sister's missing. Some man's been hanging around watching her—'

'I can assure you we'll be sending some officers to inspect the property you've told us about as quickly as possible.'

'Thank you. I know I haven't called 999 but it *is* urgent. She's also three months pregnant.' I should have mentioned that in the first place. 'Does that make any difference to how quickly you can get there?'

'I've added that information to the notes and it will be passed on to the attending officers.'

I close my eyes. I'll just have to get back around there myself.

'If I could take an address for yourself please?'

'My home address? But I'm not there right now.'

'The address you're calling from then, assuming you're intending to stay there.' The man's voice is infuriatingly passive. 'Another unit will attend to get some more details from you.'

'Like what? I've told you everything.'

'We may need a photo. And as you said, you're currently with Tamara's husband. So we'll need to speak with him.'

Great. He'll probably tell them about her note. However, I've no choice other than to reel their address off. I drop into the armchair as I end the call, already knowing that I can't just hang around here, waiting for the police to show up.

'At least they're doing *something*.' Dale leans onto the back of the sofa. 'You did make it all sound pretty bad. When you put it all together like that, I mean.'

'It *is* bad.' I stand again. I can't keep still. Then, sensing the weight of someone looking in as they walk past, I storm to the window and draw the curtains across again. No wonder Tamara constantly feels like she's under surveillance here. I point at the huge window. 'Have you ever thought about getting blinds? It's like being in a goldfish bowl.'

'Did they say anything about who the car belongs to?'

'The police aren't going to tell *me*, are they?'

'Look, there's nothing you can do here, Ali. Why don't you go home and I'll call you when there's any news.'

Hmmm. He's probably trying to get rid of me so he can go grovelling to that tart over the road. 'I'm going nowhere until I know my sister's safe. Besides, the police are supposed to be calling round here.'

'I thought you and Wayne had plans this weekend.' He really *is* trying to get rid of me.

'Unless she gets back soon, I'll probably call my plans off.' My heart sinks at this snap decision I've made but Wayne will understand.

'I can't just wait around here.' I reach into my bag for my keys. 'I'm going back.'

'To the cottage?'

'Yeah, I've got to. I've got a really bad feeling. It's been niggling at me ever since we drove away.'

'Wait. I'm coming too.'

'You should wait here for the police.'

'She's my wife.'

'Yeah. When it suits you.' I let a long breath out. 'Alright, since you want to come with me, have you got something we can force the door with if she doesn't answer again?'

'We can't do that.'

'I'll do it myself if you won't help me.'

'I've got some tools in the boot. There's a metal tyre lever that might do the job.'

'Good. Right, let's go then. As I head back through the hallway, I fire a text off to Wayne.

I'm worried sick about her. Police are going to where we think she might be, but they said it could take them up to two hours. So I'm heading back there with Dale. It's in the middle of nowhere and there's no signal. I'll let you know as soon as I can. x

Where exactly are you going, love? Just so I know where you are. x

I head over to Google Maps again, drop a pin onto Poppy Cottage and send it back to him. I'm warmed by his caring where I am. And it's just as well someone else knows.

Just in case.

38

TAMARA

THE KETTLE CLICKS off in the kitchen and the air is thick with the smell of toast. Just a few minutes ago, I thought I was going to get something to eat and drink. But my stress levels have now rocketed so high, I probably wouldn't get anything down anyway. I certainly wouldn't keep anything down.

'You might be interested in these photos, Tamara?' Rachel pushes against my shoulder and I fall backwards onto the sofa. My eye falls on the fire poker laid on the hearth. If only that had been there last night, I might have been able to fight my way out of here. But it's here *now* and depending on how things progress over the next few minutes, I won't hesitate to swing it at one or both of them to get myself free.

She hands me her phone. My first instinct now I've got it in my hand is to call 999 until I see the *no service* message at the top.

'Look at the photos.' Her voice is sterner as she points at her phone.

'What is it?' A picture of some clothes thrown on a carpet blurs in front of my eyes. 'What am I supposed to be looking at?'

'If you look closely, you'll see they're a mixture of *my* clothes – and Dale's. And it's *your* bedroom carpet.'

I peer more closely, realising with a sickening thud that she's telling the truth. Oh my God, she's been in my bedroom.

'Keep swiping right.' Her voice is almost a purr. I don't want to see any more but something compels me to. I guess I need to know. I'd been avoiding sex with Dale until I'd had the scan as I've been so scared of it risking a miscarriage. So evidently, he went elsewhere.

'You might recognise your bed in that one.'

Martin drops into an armchair. 'I'm sorry you're having to look at those,' he says. 'I do know exactly how you feel.'

After all he's done, he's acting sympathetically towards me now. He's as much a psycho as she is.

Dale's fast asleep and naked on our bed. The photo is time and date stamped, this morning at 2:28 am. So while I was trying to survive in that dreadful cellar, my husband was tucked up in bed with *her*.

'You're an absolute slut,' I hiss. How the hell did I end up living across the road from such a bitch?

'Now, now, Tamara – this can't have come as a complete shock to you.'

'You must know he won't leave me for you. Not when I'm having his baby.'

'So you'd stay with him, even though he's been having an affair with *me*.' She shakes her head and pulls a face as though I'm the most pitiful creature she's ever set eyes on. 'Talk about having no dignity.'

'How long has it been going on?' I feel winded. Like it really matters how long it's been going on. He's done it again – that's all that counts.

'*Long* before your baby was ever heard of.'

I stare back at her. 'I don't believe you.'

Surely he wouldn't be so callous? Not when I was going

through the whole IVF rigmarole? She snatches the phone out of my hand and presses on the screen. 'Here.' She thrusts it back at me. There's a photo of him poking his head from what looks like our ensuite shower, clearly having been caught unawares, then another of him standing naked in our kitchen. There's a packing box beside him so we must have only just moved in. Sure enough, it's date and timestamped again. 16th September, 11:31 am. I'd have been at work at that time. The bastard.

So six months after I caught him out with his colleague and he begged me for another chance, he's back to his old tricks again. Not to mention the *huge* affair he had a few years ago when he'd actually planned to leave me for her.

'He wants to leave you.' It's like she's read my mind as she bends to retrieve her phone from me. 'The only thing that's keeping him there is the *baby*.' She pulls a face as she says the word. 'Is that what you want? To trap him there when it's not *you* he's even staying for?'

I stare back at her pinched face and narrowed eyes. To think I could have ever thought she was pretty. 'What do you want me to say?'

To be honest I'm too shocked to react. After my overnight ordeal, I've barely got any fight left in me for myself, let alone for Dale. Whenever I've had to deal with confrontational situations in the past, I've been pumped up and raring to go, ready to wipe the floor with whoever was getting in my way. I need to find some of that within myself again, and I need to find it sharpish. I daren't look over at the poker. I don't want to draw attention to it.

'You need to take a long, hard look at yourself, Tamara.' Anger prickles at the back of my neck as she leans forward and prods at my chest. 'Haven't you got any self-respect? Surely you can't be thinking of staying with him after seeing those photos.'

'She's with *me* now,' Martin says. 'So I'll look after her.'

Anger becomes nausea. I'm now locked up in this house with not one but *two* unhinged maniacs. But I've got to keep calm for the baby's sake. However, that poker is going to get me out of this. He can't have realised he's left it there. I'm watching *her* every move as well. She's far too close to me and has such menace in her eyes, she could be capable of anything. I reach to my left and drag a pillow across my middle. I've never got to this three-month stage before. I can't lose this baby now. I'll do *anything* not to lose it.

'You should know I'll stop at nothing until Dale's with me.' Rachel's voice is a snarl as she towers over me.

I'd love to tell her that she can't give him what he really wants, the baby he's always wanted. She's got at least ten years on me, but I don't want to anger her any further by reminding her of this. She drops her phone into her pocket and her fingers curl into a fist at her side. So I'll tell her what she wants to hear.

39

TAMARA

'You're welcome to each other,' I say. Perhaps I'm beginning to mean this, or am I just saying it to throw her off guard? I'm still not certain I even believe her. She's clearly a complete bunny boiler, so she could have got into our house and staged those photos. They don't offer definitive proof that they've been sleeping together. Although even I know it doesn't look good.

'You know I'll take care of you,' Martin reaffirms. 'Since he's now shown you what he's made of.'

'Just let me out of here.' I press the cushion into myself. 'I can't take any more after being locked in that cellar all night. Please, just let me go.'

'You've been locked up all night in the *cellar?*' Rachel's jaw drops and she spins around to Martin. 'What happened? That wasn't really the plan, was it?'

'Things went wrong, like I told you.' He looks down at his feet, his voice low. 'And I didn't know about her baby.' His head jerks up again. 'It was a shock, alright? But, anyway, I think I've got my head around things now.'

What's that supposed to mean? Oh God, he's looking at me with a manic look in his eyes. What's he going to do?

He drops forward onto the carpet. I hold my breath as he shuffles across the floor towards me and tugs the cushion away from my midriff.

'*I'll* be your baby's Daddy.' I grimace as he lays his head on my knee and rests his palm across my stomach. 'I've had all night to think and I'm sure this could work. I've always wanted to be a dad so this could be my chance.' His warped face breaks into a smile. 'I swear it to you, sweetheart, I'll *never* hurt you. In fact, the two of you will never want for *anything.*'

'I just want to go home.' I press my back into the sofa, trying to shrink back from the weight of his hand. 'Please! I don't feel too good.' I'm not lying. It might just be stress but my stomach feels even more crampy than before. I'm longing just to lay out on my bed at home but who knows where home is going to end up for me after what I've seen in those photos.

'You need to accept that you and Dale are over,' Rachel repeats. 'I really can't understand why he's stayed with you for so long. You should see him when he's around me, he lights up – he becomes a different person. One who smiles and has fun.' Her smile vanishes and her face hardens again. 'You, you're dragging him down to where you are, with your neediness, your bad memories, your feeling sick, your insecurities...' Her voice trails off.

That's quite a list. The thing is, it's all true. I've been existing rather than living for so long.

'Is that what he's told you?' Misery pools at my centre. I know he has. He told me in the throes of an argument when he was late home a few weeks ago that I'm dragging him down. That I depress him. How could I have thought things might have taken a turn for the better? How could I have ever imagined that Dale would plan a Valentine's surprise for me? If only I could turn the clock back to yesterday and do everything differently.

Martin shuffles as close as he can get to my feet. If it was any other human, I'd probably enjoy the warmth against my still-chilled legs after my night in the cellar. But his proximity is setting my teeth on edge.

'Please move your hand.' I push it off. 'Like I said, I don't feel well.' I can't bear his fingers on me. I can't bear him anywhere near me.

Thankfully, he does as I ask, but hauls himself from the floor and sits right beside me. 'You're my second chance, Tamara,' he says, reaching for my hand. 'With you, I can put everything right.'

I want to scream at him to leave me alone but don't want to risk being forced back into that cellar. Or worse. Where I am gives me an opportunity. Either to make some noise if my sister returns to the door or to grab that fire poker as soon as the opportunity presents itself.

'At least you won't be hanging around the street any more like a lovesick puppy,' Rachel laughs as she looks at Martin.

'I can't believe you would treat someone like this,' I say. 'You and him.' I jerk my head to the left. 'This whole *Valentine* thing.'

'You certainly left the way clear for me last night,' her laughter pauses. 'Not to mention your side of the bed.'

I swallow. All I care about is being allowed to leave. 'When are you going to let me go?' We're going around and around in ever-decreasing circles here. Rachel wants Dale. Martin wants me and I just want to get out of here. 'Like I said, you're welcome to him. I'll go and stay with my sister. But *please,* just let me leave.'

She opens her mouth to speak but before she can answer, the sound of a car engine vibrates from outside.

This is my chance.

40

ALI

At first I think I'm seeing things as we pull up. 'Isn't that your neighbour's car?' I noticed her attractive scarlet Mini Cooper on the drive earlier. It *must* be hers. With its distinctive Union Jack taillights, who else would it belong to? The question is, what the hell would she be doing *here* at my sister's last known whereabouts?

'I think it is.' There can be no denying that Dale looks as shocked as me that it's here. The situation's getting weirder by the second. Maybe it's *Rachel* who's been stalking Tamara. Perhaps while hidden in the shadows, Tamara's mistaken her for a man. I really don't know what else to think.

'Let's just get in there.' I slam the car door and rush up the path to the cottage doorway to try the handle again. It's still locked. But at least with the bitch from over the road in there, I stand a better chance of getting inside to check if my sister's safe. I knock and ring the doorbell, pausing as I hear something from inside. I'm almost certain it was my sister's voice.

'She's in there, I know she is.' I keep my finger on the doorbell. Dale looks like he's seen a ghost and clearly has about as

189

much idea as I have of how his wife and his bit on the side have ended up under the same roof in the middle of nowhere.

'Ali, I'm in here.' Tamara's voice is muffled towards the end of her sentence as though someone's holding something over her face.

I have to get in there – she's in trouble, I just know she is. I glance towards the window to the left of the door. The curtains remain tightly closed. I return to the door and bend to the letterbox.

'Open this door *now*.' I bang on it, much harder this time. 'I know you're in there, Rachel.'

Nobody replies and still, nobody comes. I kick it. Again and again. 'Get that tyre thing from the car.' I point at the boot where Dale put his toolbox as we left their house.

'We're going to get in there within the next couple of minutes,' I shout. We should have just forced the door in the first place instead of giving Rachel any sort of warning.

'Who's *we*?' Ah, so the bitch is finally answering me. She sounds like she's right on the other side of the door.

'Tamara's sister. I'm with Dale.' I bang again. 'Open this door or I swear—'

'What are you doing here?'

'Just bloody let us in.'

Silence. Is she ignoring us or is she considering opening up?

'The police won't be long, you know.' Maybe that will sway her. It's got to be easier than forcing the door.

'You've called the *police*?' Then, after another agonising pause, there's a clunk at the other side of the door as she finally unlocks it. Just in case she has any thoughts of using a door chain, the second the door's ajar, I throw my weight behind it and send her flying backwards.

'Where's my sister?' I storm towards her and slam her into the wall.

'I'm in here.' I could weep with relief at the sound of Tamara's voice. She's safe and we've got in to her. 'Make sure she doesn't try to leave,' I order Dale as Rachel attempts to compose herself.

I dart into the room where Tamara's perched at the edge of a sofa, her arms wrapped around her belly. I lunge at her and wrap her in my arms.

'I've been so worried about you. Are you alright? What has she done to you? Is the baby OK?'

She's weeping too hard to answer my barrage of questions.

'Calm down and talk to me. I need to know what she's done to you.'

Then I notice *him*. A man. Probably *the* man. Her *stalker*. He's skulking in the corner by the window. 'What the hell have you two done to her?'

'Nothing, I swear to you.' He stammers. 'I was only trying to look after her.' To be fair, despite his size, he doesn't look the sort to have inflicted much harm if appearances can be judged in this sort of situation. He almost looks too docile. 'I only *ever* wanted to look after her.'

'So it's *you* that's been hanging around our house?' Dale storms across the room and grabs the man by the scruff of his neck. 'I don't care what's gone on in the past, you don't get to terrify my wife half to death like you've done.'

'*What's gone on in the past?* What's that supposed to mean?'

Ignoring my question, Dale rams him up against the fireplace, bending him backwards into the wall. 'You know my wife's pregnant, don't you?'

'Your *wife*.' Rachel's voice is acidic as she appears in the doorway.

'I thought I told you not to leave her unattended,' I shout at Dale.

'You weren't bothered about *your wife* last night, were you?' Rachel's tone is laced with poison.

'We agreed that was it, didn't we?' Dale relaxes his hold on the man as they pant into each other's faces. 'I never wanted to see your face *again*. What the hell are you playing at?'

'So you two *know* each other?' I shriek as Tamara stiffens in my arms. 'What's going on?'

Dale twists to look at Tamara. 'I'll explain everything, love. Let's just get you home first.'

'How could you let this happen to her?' I let my sister go and rise from the sofa. 'I think you need to let me look after her from here.'

'I've been locked up in a cellar while he's been in bed with that slag over there.' She's rocking forwards and back on the sofa, in a similar way to how she did when the shit hit the fan when we were kids. Her lips are white with what could be either cold or terror. Or both.

'You've been *what*?'

'All night.' She rocks herself even harder.

'Don't you ever call me a *slag*.'

I throw myself in front of Rachel before she can get to Tamara.

'The police will be here at any moment.' Dale's voice is a low growl. 'Before they arrive, I need to know how the hell you all came to be here together like this. Rachel?'

41

ALI

'Is that all you care about? Getting to the bottom of things?' I swing around to face my brother-in-law. 'What about your poor wife?'

'I don't want him anywhere near me,' Tamara says through gritted teeth. 'Not after what he's done.'

'What the hell have you told her?' Dale was pale enough before but now... Then, from the corner of my eye, I notice the man edging towards the door.

'Stay where you bloody are,' I yell as I launch myself in front of it to prevent him from leaving. I glance around to see if there's anything I can swing at him and my eyes fall on what looks like a fire poker in the fireplace. A belt on the head with that would stop someone in their tracks.

'I've seen the photos of you both,' Tamara continues with more conviction in her voice this time. 'I don't even know what you're doing here, Dale. Just leave me alone, will you?'

'I was worried about—'

'You can come back with me, sis.' I retake my place beside her, silently daring Rachel to come anyway near. 'But we need to get you and the baby checked over before we speak to the police.'

'The *baby*,' Rachel snorts. 'I'm sick of hearing about it.'

'What photos?' Dale's voice is as hard as nails as he looks from Tamara to Rachel. 'And how the hell did you know where Tamara was anyway? That's what I want to know.'

'You've done it to me *again*, haven't you?' Tamara says. 'All this time, you've been telling me I'm paranoid. How could you do this to me? To our baby?'

I rest my arm around the back of her shoulders. 'You don't need him anymore,' I tell her. 'Me, Wayne and the boys – we're your family. We'll look after you both.'

'I honestly didn't know about the baby.' The man edges closer to the door since I've moved out of the way.

Dale darts in front of it. 'I hope you're not getting any daft ideas about doing a runner,' he says. 'Because you're going nowhere.'

'It was all *her*.' He points at Rachel, '*She* told me Tamara wanted me to arrange something – that she felt the same way as I did.'

'What the *fuck* is all this?' Dale says, the word *fuck* making Tamara jump. Her skinny shoulders are shaking. 'I *helped* you once, and this is how you repay me? You come after *my* wife?'

'You need to get her away from him. He'll only ever hurt her, he will.' The man's talking to me as he nods towards Dale. 'He went with my wife too, and well, he'll obviously go with anything that moves.'

'He went with *your* wife? Dale did? What are you talking about?' I just don't understand what's going on here. There are evidently things I know absolutely nothing about.

'Dale was with Martin's wife – six years ago.' Rachel's voice is smug as she replies to me. 'And look what happened to *her*.'

So the man now has a name – *Martin*. 'What do you mean?'

Tamara jumps to her feet. 'I need to go upstairs.'

'What's the matter? Are you alright?' It's a stupid question.

'I'm bleeding,' she gasps. 'I can feel it. I need to check.' She turns towards the door and I jump up after her.

'Get out of our way,' I snarl at Dale and Martin who've formed a wall in front of us. 'I need to look after my sister.'

I steer her past them and out into the hallway. She looks more fragile than I've ever seen her and the sooner I get her and the baby checked over, the better. 'You're safe now. The baby will be too, I promise.' I shouldn't say this. How *can* I promise such a thing? I've actually lost count of the number of miscarriages she's endured. All she's ever wanted is to create her own family. A happier one than the family which was forced onto us as children.

'I only wanted to look after you,' the man shouts after us. What an absolute weirdo. He's followed her around, stalked her, lured her to this cottage with some note and locked her in a cellar all night. God knows what else he might have done to her. We'll find out about that soon enough. For now, the baby has to take priority.

'We'll go straight to the hospital,' I say. 'Come on, into the car.' I glance at the door, still slightly ajar. We need to get out of here before anyone thinks to lock it again.

'I can't wait.' She breaks away from me and calls back over her shoulder as she rushes up the stairs, her voice wobbling. 'I need to know if I'm losing my baby.'

'She isn't, is she?' Dale appears in the doorway of the lounge and pulls it behind him, still holding onto the handle, presumably so no one else can follow him out. They sound like they're too busy arguing between themselves in there anyway.

'I'm going to drive her straight to the hospital. But *you,* you can stay away for now. She doesn't need any more stress.'

A door slams above us. Martin's and Rachel's voices have risen from the lounge but I don't care what's going on now. I just need to get my sister out of this place and I can't believe she's stalling things by going up to the bathroom.

'I'm not leaving her – you heard her – she's bleeding.'

'You gave up all your rights as a husband when you jumped into bed yet again with someone else. You've done more than enough damage.'

'It wasn't *me* who trapped her in a house overnight.' He storms towards me. 'I haven't caused this.'

'No, but it was your girlfriend who was in on it all. Who cooked up some sort of sick plan to presumably get Tamara out of the way.'

'She's not my girlfriend.' He steps in front of me and lowers himself to sit on the stairs. 'Look, that's my baby Tamara's carrying. I've got a right to come to the hospital with you both.'

'You've got *no* rights after how you've treated her.'

'Why are you being like this *now*? You were OK with me on the journey here.'

'Things have moved on since then, don't you think? I've learned a few more things since we got here.'

Tamara appears on the stairs, tears streaming down her face. 'There's blood,' she sobs. 'I'm losing the baby. It's as if I'm being punished.'

42

TAMARA

DALE RUSHES up the stairs to me, his arms outstretched. As if I'm going to just fall into them. 'Come on, love, it's probably nothing. A bit of blood doesn't necessarily mean you're losing the baby.'

He catches hold of my arm and I wrench it away. 'Just leave me alone, will you?' I can't stand to have him anywhere near me.

Ali drops her keys onto the hallway table and offers her hand as I reach the bottom of the stairs. 'Let's get you in the car, sis. Come on.'

Clutching my stomach as if that can make any difference to the outcome, I stumble towards her. 'I don't even know if there's any point going to the hospital.' My voice is a wail as a cramp shoots through me. 'I've got the awful pains again – it's the same as before.'

'What's going on?' Martin appears in the lounge door with Rachel trying to peer around him.

'Just get her things for her,' Ali turns to him. 'Now.'

'Mind your own business, you loser.' Dale snatches Ali's keys up and strides towards the front door before pausing there. 'Don't think this is over, Sanders. As soon as my wife's been checked over, you're going to get it.' He storms out, presumably towards my sister's car.

Ali lets go of my arm and lunges after Dale. 'I said you're *not* coming with us. Get back in here. '

'I'll get your things.' As Martin disappears up the stairs, I edge towards the safety of the open door. Ali might be going after Dale but I can't believe she's left me alone in the house again. All they've got to do is slam this door and lock it and I'm back to square one. But this time I'm losing my baby. I can't believe this is happening. Not again.

Rachel steps from the lounge, looking at me like I'm something she's stepped in. 'Never mind, eh? Everything happens for a reason, doesn't it?'

'Shut your vile mouth.'

'What baby would want to be born into what's left of your shitty marriage anyway?' A ghost of a smile plays on her lips.

I stare back at her. I know she hates me but how can she be so cruel?

'It's too bad about your womb problems, but I guess the way is even clearer for me and Dale now. No baby and all that.'

As a car door slams outside, I barge past her, sending her flying into the door frame as I go after the one thing that will punish her for how she's destroyed my life.

'What the hell are you playing at?' Rachel comes after me. 'You're supposed to be leaving with your sister, aren't you?'

My sights are set on only one thing now. After what she and Dale have done, I don't care what happens anymore. All I can see is a gaping black hole where my future should have been. Everything's gone and I might as well be dead. I've been here before, but I care even less this time. All I know is that she's going to pay. And she isn't the only one.

I rush towards the fireplace and grab the fire poker, raising it into the air, before tapping it a couple of times against my other palm. For a split second, all is calm as Rachel and I face each other, apart from the continued shouting outside between Dale and Ali.

'Yeah, and what are you going to do with that?'

'You've no idea what I'm capable of, especially since I've nothing left to lose.' Maybe I'll get away with this. Maybe I won't. I could argue it was self-defence. I could also argue I was maddened by my hormones.

Rachel sucks a sharp breath in. 'You wouldn't dare.'

'You've taken everything from me.'

'Come on, just put it down.' It's a pleasure to watch her smug smile be replaced with an expression of uncertainty and fear. 'You hit me with that and you'll do time. You know that, don't you?'

'It'll be more than worth it.' I need to end this before she tries to make a run for it. Or before someone comes back into the room and tries to stop me. I hold the poker aloft.

She begins to back away, not that there's much room behind her. 'This is going too far now. Please just put it down, Tamara.'

As if her use of my name could bring me to my senses. If anything, it riles me even more. I whip the poker through the air, and with a dull thud, it strikes the side of Rachel's head. Blood spurts into the air as she staggers into the wall. Somewhere in the distance, I can still hear my husband and sister shouting at each other but they sound even further away now. *I just want her dead. I just want her dead. I just want her dead.* I raise the poker back above my head as her knees begin to buckle.

'No stop.' Martin rushes into the room.

'Happy Valentine's, bitch,' I screech as I bring the poker crashing onto Rachel's head again for a second time. Her arms flail in all directions as she slumps to the floor. Our eyes meet, hers wide with agony as she rests on her knees. Her body collapses forward at my feet. Bile rises to my throat as I turn away from my handiwork, tears burning in my eyes.

I somehow knew being held against my will in this house would end in tragedy but never dreamed my husband would be such an instigator of it.

Martin stands with his mouth wide open as he stares at her. 'Oh my God, what have you done?' He clasps his hand to his mouth. 'Is she...? Have you...?'

I can't reply. I can't even speak. All that's just happened is somewhat de-ja-vu. Apart from the stomach cramps and the fact that I'm having yet another miscarriage, it's like I'm back there again. In the hallway of that former farmhouse, staring at the body slumped in front of the fire.

'It's like it's happening all over again.' Martin drops to his knees beside Rachel, his voice a low moan as he echoes my thinking. 'It's the same. It's all exactly the same.' He goes to touch her but before his hand connects, he withdraws it as if he can't bear to.

I can't take my eyes off Rachel. It's no wonder Martin's thinking of Belinda as he crouches beside her. She's landed on the floor in the exact same position as Belinda ended up in. Pose of the child, in yoga speak. How ironic. Her blonde, blood-matted hair flops forward across the floor. If images of the two women were to be placed side by side, we could have a game of spot the difference.

'That's what they get when they think they can take what's mine.' I stare at her, wanting to check her pulse. I want to know if I've been as successful as last time but somehow, I'm both in shock and in awe of what I've done and I'm rooted to the spot.

'What do you mean?' He rests back on his heels.

I want to see the look on his face when I tell him it was me who ended his wife's life. 'What do you think I mean? Rachel, Belinda – they both had it coming.'

The expression on Martin's face as he stares at me could curdle milk. 'It was *you*?' His lip curls in hatred. 'My wife? Belinda? *You* did it?'

'And I'd do it all over again.'

'I wanted to set you free. But you're nothing but an evil—'

'And you're nothing but a deluded bastard. Belinda didn't want you and neither do I.'

'I thought her death was all my fault.' Martin's eyes glisten with tears. 'I've spent six years believing I was a murderer after I pushed her.'

'Well, you won't have to worry about that any more.' I hold the poker aloft as his eyes widen in the same way Rachel's just did. Before he can get enough balance on his knees to raise his arms in self-defence, the metal poker is once again slicing through the air and I hear my sister's voice in the doorway.

But Martin won't be telling anyone what I've just confessed to. Not now. Not ever.

43

ALI

TAMARA SLAMS the lounge door and lurches past me in the hallway. 'Come on then, let's go.' She darts towards the car like she's got the devil after her.

'What the hell were you doing in there?' The gravel crunches beneath my trainers as I twist to go after her.

'Please Ali, let's get out of here.'

'Didn't he give you your things?' Just as she's getting into the car, I notice her empty hands.'

'Just drive.' We slam our doors at the same time.

'You're not supposed to be coming with us.' I glance back at Dale.

'Please, Ali.' Tamara also checks behind us, presumably to check that neither of them are coming after her. I start the engine.

'What the hell's going on?' Dale echoes my question. 'Has something else happened in there?'

'Just go. *Now!*' She makes my ears ring as she yells the last word. I ram the car into gear, glaring at her as we set off. She's got every right to be upset but no right to shout at me. I've only ever tried to help her.

'Hang on.' I screech the car back to a halt, even though we've barely got a few feet away from the cottage. 'What on earth is that all over you? Is it *blood?*'

Dale hangs between the front seats to get a closer look at her as well.

'Oh my God, sis. What happened in there? What did they do to you?'

'I hit back, that's all. It was self-defence.' The tears have stopped and an air of something else entirely seems to have washed over my sister. 'People keep thinking they can do what they want to me, but they can't. As I've just shown them.'

'Is it *your* blood?' She doesn't look to be hurt, apart from what's happening inside her. Which begs the question, if it isn't her blood, what exactly *has* she shown them?

'Just drive, will you.'

'Not until you tell me what's happened.' Panic rises from my stomach into my throat. The police are on their way and my sister's covered in blood. 'Was there some sort of fight?'

'Do I have to drive this thing myself?' She leans towards me and screams into my ear. 'I just want to go home.'

I force the car back into gear and the tyres screech as I set off along the single-track road. My sister breaks into loud sobs at the side of me. It's going to take some serious therapy to get her through this, especially if she is losing the baby. As far as I know, there are only one or two embryos left. She's going to be in pieces if the worst is happening.

'I thought we were heading straight for the hospital?' Dale says. 'Now you're saying you want to go home?'

'There's no point.' Her voice is calmer now the car's in motion. 'Please just take me home. I know the signs. There's nothing they can do to prevent the inevitable.

'There must be *something* they can do.' I reach across to my sister's blood-splattered hand, but she jerks it away from me.'

'Just leave me alone, eh? I just can't take anymore.'

'Tell me what happened, Tamara. I should never have left you in there – not for a second. I'm so sorry.' It dawns on me then that if anything *bad* has happened, I'll have the stain of someone's blood on my conscience. All because I was too busy having a go at Dale and trying to prevent him from travelling back with us.

'The bitch had it coming. She was laughing at me.'

'Had *what* coming?' Dale leans forward between the seats again. 'Is that *Rachel's* blood?' He's doing his best to make his voice sound nonchalant. As if he doesn't care that his bit on the side could have been knocked out, or whatever happened while we were bickering outside.

'*His* blood too.' She sits back in her seat and folds her arms as if to stop them from shaking. She was bad enough before but the trembling is even more violent now. 'They can't get away with what they've done to me.'

'What did you hit them with?' Really, I know without asking that it must be what I saw in the fireplace – it has to be. There was nothing else in that room.

'The fire poker.'

I glance at her again. She looks almost pleased with herself. 'If you'd have heard what she said to me to provoke me.' Her voice shakes.

'What *did* she say?'

'*What baby would want to be born into your shitty marriage anyway?*' She mimics Rachel's high-pitched voice. 'I was forced to shut her up.' She's staring forward, a look of defiance on her face. My usually angst-ridden and people-pleasing sister has been replaced by someone wild and dangerous.

'What do you mean, *you shut her up*?' Oh my God, who knows what she's done back there?

She twists in her seat and jerks her thumb in the direction we've just travelled from. 'She doesn't deserve to go on wrecking people's lives.'

'What is it you're saying?' Dale's voice rises to what must be the top of its range.

'Why do you care so much?' Tamara shrieks. 'None of it would have happened if it wasn't for *you*.'

'If you've whacked both of them with a fire poker, we should call for an ambulance,' I tell her. 'We can't just leave them there.'

44

ALI

As I continue to drive, my conscience and my anger wrestle with each other. The human in me says we should stop; we should go back or at the very least, call for help. But whatever we *should* do, I keep driving anyway.

'What are you doing, Ali?' Dale asks. 'I thought you were turning around?'

'Why would I want to return to help the people who've ruined my sister's life?' I've been driving at a tortoise's pace through the mist since we left the cottage, but now I squeeze the accelerator closer to the floor. 'Besides, the police are on their way. They'll help them when they get there.' That's how I'll justify it to myself if it slinks back to haunt me over the coming months.

'They said it could be *two hours* from when we called them. We need to go back now.' Dale's voice is filled with panic. Me, I feel strangely calm.

We travel in silence for a few more moments.

'Are you really not going to turn around?' Dale is beginning to sound more desperate. It seems he cares more about the woman he's been messing around with than I first suspected.

'The police will sort them out,' I repeat. I'm totally matter of fact. Who knows what Wayne will make of me driving away from people who could be badly injured? Perhaps, if I'm honest, part of me can't bear to see what my little sister might have inflicted and what she might be capable of.

'*You* go back if you really want to.' I jump as Tamara twists in her seat to shout at Dale. 'Stop the car, Ali. Let him out.'

I ignore her and keep driving. She needs a hospital, no matter what she says.

'You've ruined everything, you absolute bastard.' She twists in her seat as she throws her fist in Dale's direction but misses as he shifts himself to the driver's side of the back seat. 'You've done it again, haven't you? It's *your* fault I'm losing this baby. And it's *your* fault I was forced to hit them both with the fire poker.' Then suddenly, all fight seems to drain from her as she drops her head into her hands and sobs.

I should stop, I should comfort her but, we're still a good twenty minutes from the hospital. I'm out of my depth here and don't know what to do for the best.

Dale reaches through the seats and squeezes her shoulder.

'Get your hands off me.' She twists her shoulder out of his grasp.

'I'm so sorry.' He pulls his arm back. 'I don't know what else you want me to say.'

'Sorry?' The way she roars with laughter is one of the most awful sounds I've ever heard. 'You couldn't have caused any more damage if you'd tried.'

'It sounds to me like it's *you* who's caused the damage this time.' His tone is firmer now.

She drops her head back into her hands. 'It's all right for you – you'll be able to go back home,' – her sobbing resumes, – 'and carry on with the rest of your life, but when the police find out I lost it like that and attacked them, it's all over for me.'

'Look, no matter what's happened in there, we've got your

back.' He brings his hand forward again and rests it on her shoulder. 'We could tell the police there was a fight and they did it to *each other*.'

I give him a look in the rear-view mirror as if to say, *how stupid can you get*? If we're going to do or say something to protect her, we need to come up with something better than that.

But this sudden allegiance brings Tamara's sobs to a halt and she lifts her head again. '*Would* you really say that?' Then she lets out a wail. 'So why have you done what you've done to our marriage? We were having a baby. I thought we were happy.' She wipes a glob of snot from under her nose. 'Why have you done this to us – *again*?' I'd say she's got worse things to worry about right now but I'll let her have her moment of lamenting Dale's affair.

I ease off the single-track road back onto an ordinary stretch of tarmac with a huge sigh of relief. Houses and shops appear all around us, and I can almost pretend everything's normal as we journey further and further away from whatever my sister has inflicted on Martin and Rachel.

I'm trying to sideline that we've left two people in God-only-knows-what sort of a state back there. But I can't pretend that my sister isn't sprayed with someone else's blood as she rides beside me. It's probably better to let her get herself cleaned up before we go anywhere near the hospital. More cars start to pass us on the other side of the road as we get closer and closer to reality. And then, a police car.

'Oh my God.' Tamara claps her hand over her mouth as she turns to see where they're going. 'They've just turned off that way. They're going to find them, they're going to bloody find them.'

'It's OK, it's all going to be OK.' Dale reaches for her hand. 'Nothing's going to happen to you.'

'How can you say that?'

His voice is low and calm. 'Because me and you are going to get away from here for a few days. It's the least I can do after what I've put you through.'

'Just like that?' I shake my head. 'You can't just disappear.'

'We'll go home, we'll get you cleaned up and then—'

'The police will probably be at your house by now, remember? And if they see the state of her, they'll arrest her on the spot. They'll probably arrest *all* of us. We're complicit here. We know they've been clouted with the fire poker.'

'They were both out cold when I left the room.' Tamara's voice is small yet strangely calm. 'Dale's right. I do need to get away from here.'

'You'd better come to my house for a shower,' I tell her. 'The police were heading to yours to take statements from us.'

'But that implicates you.' I can sense her eyes on me. 'I don't want to drag you any further into this.'

'I'm already dragged in.' I stop myself from adding, *whether I like it or not*, and breathe another sigh of relief as I turn in the direction of my village. I'll let her shower, I'll lend her some clothes, and then I'll have to send her on her way with Dale. He's right, it seems to be the only option. We've already reported her missing so she'll just stay missing. I'll tell the police that Dale's still looking for her.

'I'll just lie low for a few days,' she says. 'Until we know exactly what damage I've caused. You can just tell the police you still haven't seen me.'

'But Rachel or Martin are bound to tell—'

'I can't think about them right now,' she replies. 'I just need to get cleaned up and to get away. You promise you'll help me?' She turns to look at Dale. 'I've no phone with me, no payment cards, nothing.'

'Does this mean there's a chance you'll forgive me?'

'I can't think straight right now.'

She's been through so much, my sister – our childhood,

Dale's affairs, the loss of seven pregnancies over the last few years and now what she's been through this Valentine's weekend of hell. She's barmy to be running away with Dale, but he's probably the only person who can bring some normality into her life right now, at least until she comes to terms with the loss of this latest pregnancy. If she were to be arrested and locked up for attacking them both *now*, I dread to think what it could do to her state of mind. If Rachel or Martin *do* lead the police to her, a few days to prepare herself beforehand could make all the difference to how she handles it.

Now all I've got to do is figure out how to get Tamara into the house to shower without being seen by the children – or by Wayne.

45

WAYNE

'You could at least tell me whether it's a man or a woman. *Please!*' I won't rest until I know for certain that whatever they're examining in that tent isn't my wife's body. I should never have let her come here and I should have got here faster to look for her. 'I need to know what's going on, please!'

'We really can't tell you anything, sir.' The officer looks apologetic. 'Not at this stage. I'm so sorry.'

'Dad, what's happened?' Edward steps from the car. 'Where's Mum?'

'You really need to get your children away from here,' the officer says. 'Like I've already told you, this is a crime scene.'

'Back in the car, Edward.' I point at it. 'Now.' The officer's right. They shouldn't be with me but what else was I supposed to do with them? Ali should have been back an hour ago.

'What makes you think you might know someone inside there?' He jerks his head in the direction of the cottage.

'My wife sent me this as the location she was heading to.' I tug my phone from my pocket and open Ali's previous text message. 'She dropped a pin on the map so I'd know where she was going. To some degree, she must have felt something was unsafe to have sent me this in the first place.'

'If you could write your details down, one of my colleagues will need to speak to you.'

'They can speak to me now, can't they?'

'We can't do it *here*, but someone will visit your home to take a full statement.'

I accept the notepad from him and write my name and number. 'We'll need to take your address too,' he says. 'And can I just ask, what time your wife was heading here?'

I check my watch. 'It'll be more than a couple of hours ago,' I tell him.

'Was she alone?'

'As far as I know, she was with Dale Fenton, that's our brother-in-law.' I bristle as I refer to him. He's already got a hell of a lot to answer for. I glance at the tent. But it could be *him* in there. It could be any of them. Or it might be none of them. 'Please, can't you just confirm that it isn't my wife.' She's about five foot seven and was wearing jeans, a red jumper and—' Ali's image enters my mind. I couldn't cope if anything has happened to her.

'Why was she here in the first place?'

'She was looking for her sister, that's Tamara Fenton. She's been missing overnight and it was believed she might have come here.' I gesture at the cottage. 'It had shown up on her husband's *find my phone* app.'

'I see.' He scribbles something on the notepad I've just handed back.

'My wife was really worried about her.'

'Yes, it was your wife who made the initial call to us which brought us here.'

'Dad!' Edward pokes his head from the back of the car. 'I need the toilet.'

'My colleagues have already visited the Fenton's home,' the

officer says. 'But there was no one there. So now I've got *your* home address, there'll be someone around to see you as soon as possible.'

'But—'

'I'm really sorry, Sir, but we'll hopefully be able to tell you more then.'

The car door slams and Oscar hurtles towards me this time. 'Why are we waiting, Dad? Why are you talking to the policeman?'

'Take your boys home.' The officer nods towards the car. 'We'll talk to you shortly.'

I steer Oscar back to the back seat. 'Are you both strapped in?' I feel sick. If anything's happened to Ali, I'll never forgive myself. I start the engine back up before reaching for my phone. *No service.* Shit. I just need to know that she's safe. She was right to trust her gut about her sister and I just pray with every fibre of my being that her concern hasn't dragged her into something nasty.

Whatever's happened could be somehow connected to Dale being in the pub with that woman last night. Why Tamara keeps going back to him, I'll never know, but then I suppose she was taught by the victim of all victims – her mother. It all left its mark on Ali as well but she dealt with it by having counselling and distancing herself from her parents.

'When can we see Mum?'

'She'll be home soon,' I reply, praying it's true. 'She's just helping Auntie Tamara. I'll ring her when we get near to some signal to see where she is.'

'What's signal? Can we see Auntie Tamara too? Is she still coming tonight?'

'I really don't know.' I rub at my throbbing head. It's true. I *really* don't know anything. Nor can I set the sat nav going without any signal. I just hope I can find my way around these roads in the mist.

After a few wrong turns, we eventually emerge from the single-track roads and onto a stretch where there are some houses, so I pull into a layby to check my phone. 'Yes.' Some bars of signal have finally appeared.

'Dad,' they groan in unison. 'Why are we stopping.'

'I still need the toilet,' Edward wails. 'I want to go home.'

'Just a minute – I'm just giving Mum a quick call.' The need to know my wife's OK supersedes *anything* else right now.

'Can I say hello too?'

'Soon.'

'Oh, thank God you're alright, love.' I've never welcomed the sound of my wife's voice more. She's alive, she's safe, thank God, thank God.

'Why wouldn't I be?' She sounds puzzled. 'Where are you anyway?'

'I've just driven to the cottage you sent me the pin for. I was getting worried. I'd been trying to ring you for over an hour.'

I'd better get out of the car so the boys don't hear what I'm going to say next. 'I won't be a minute, boys. I just need to talk to your mum.' They're so impressionable at the moment and prone to repeat this sort of conversation with their friends when they go online. A car whizzes past me as I lock the doors. I can't risk my kids climbing out *here.*

'Are you there *now?*'

'No, the police sent me packing. They were *everywhere.*'

'Why, what was going on?' She sounds cagey now. In fact, her tone of voice suggests she might already know more than she seems to be letting on.

'You tell me, Ali. But first, have you found your sister?'

'Yes. I've got her with me. And Dale.'

'So you're all safe.' My insides sag with relief. Not so much for my philandering brother-in-law, but obviously for my wife and also for Tamara. I know how close she and Ali are.

'She's lost the baby.' Ali's words are heavy with grief.

'Oh no. Poor Tamara.' She tries to be tough, but deep down, she just wants what we've got. A settled marriage and children. Her own family after their miserable childhood. 'Are you at the hospital with her?' That would explain why she's been out of range for far longer than she said she would be.

'No, we're at home. She's just been having a shower. She's had an awful ordeal – it's no wonder she's lost the baby.'

'What's sort of or—'. I glance at Edward and Oscar. 'Look – I'd better get back to the boys – they're scrapping on the back seat and I'm parked just off an A road. I'll be home in half an hour.'

'Make it an hour. Tamara and Dale will have gone by then so I'll be able to tell you what's happened. I don't want the boys back here until they've gone.'

I bang on the car window and shake my head at Oscar. 'Right, well you can tell me what's happened *now* then.'

'Please, Wayne, my sister needs me at the moment. I'll talk to you soon.'

'Hang on, Ali, after what I've just seen – I thought it could be *you*. They were examining a body outside that cottage.'

'What did you say?' Her tone rises. 'A body?'

'I couldn't see much – it was in a tent and a private ambulance was there as well. What the hell's happened?'

'Are you sure there was a *body*? Not just a couple of injured people?'

'Of course I'm sure. Right – you need to tell me what's been going on. *Now.*'

46

DI ROBINSON

'I THINK you'd better start at the beginning.'

I nod at my colleague as he takes a seat on the other side of our interviewees' trolley within the cubicle he's been wheeled into. 'Are you ready to take notes?'

Sergeant Bennett nods back at me.

'Are you sure you're up to this now?' The nurse who's just checked Martin's blood pressure hangs a clipboard at the end of his trolley. 'They can come back later if you're not up to it. Really, you should be still and quiet after that nasty head injury.' Her voice is brisk and businesslike.

I glare at the nurse as if to say, *let us do our bloody jobs.* It's already been a couple of hours since he was found, moaning in pain at the side of his deceased companion. We need to get whatever he remembers on record – sharpish.

'I'll be alright,' Martin says, his voice clearly weakened by his concussion. His head is wrapped in a bandage with blood seeping from the side of it, but it sounds like he's been miraculously fortunate. Especially given the state of the other casualty. 'I need to get this out of the way.'

'So what happened, Martin? You don't mind if I call you Martin, do you?'

He shakes his head but winces with the movement.

'Let's start with the incidents that have led us to what's happened today.' I use the word *us* as though I'm involved. It's a trick of mine to gain the trust of whoever I'm speaking to.

'I loved her and she tried to kill me,' Martin blurts. 'I know I shouldn't have tricked her into staying there with me but I thought she felt the same. I only wanted to look after her.'

The man's making no sense but he's clearly distraught about something. I'd better try to calm him down before the nurses kick us out of their already packed-to-the-brim accident and emergency department.

'You loved and tricked *who*? And into doing *what*, exactly?'

'I've only just discovered that she killed my wife – and I really had no idea. I'd never have let her out of that cellar if I'd known.'

'*Who* are you talking about? What do you mean?' I glance across the trolley at my colleague who looks as confused as I am. The man's talking in riddles.

He seems to shrink back into his pillows as though defeated with it all. 'Tamara Fenton killed my wife. Something snapped in me as soon as I saw Rachel slump forward on that floor back at the cottage. It was the same injury, the same position on the floor, the same blonde hair with blood dripping from it.' He closes his eyes. 'Tamara even admitted it to me – when she thought she was going to kill me too, I mean. She clearly didn't envisage me getting back up again.'

I exchange glances with Sergeant Bennett. This all sounds like it's going to take some serious unravelling. So the pregnant woman who's been reported missing is called Tamara Fenton and appears to have been held against her will for some strange reason by the man in front of us. A man whose wife was *killed* by her, or so he says. But if he's only just found this out, why was he holding her in the first place?

'Who was your wife?' We'd better get that established first.

'Belinda Sanders.' His voice is almost a whisper and he's clearly pained to say her name. 'She died almost six years ago. She was murdered. By *her*.'

I stare back at him as the facts fall into my brain like pieces of a jigsaw. That's why his face looks so familiar. Even with his bloodied bandages, I should have made the connection straight away, no matter how many new faces I encounter every week. I stood beside the man when I was a sergeant throughout his first TV appeal. I supported him as he cried for the killer of his beloved wife to be brought to justice. I passed him a tissue afterwards – he was absolutely devastated.

But two days later, we had to bring him in for questioning. I sat across the table from him when he was interviewed, albeit by my DI at the time. We had him in for over twenty-four hours, but in the end, there was no evidence whatsoever that he'd had anything to do with where Belinda Sanders ended up.

We searched his house, we searched his car, and we did a post-mortem on what was left of the body by the time it was discovered. There were no fibres, no DNA, nothing. He remained inconsolable but adamant that he'd had no involvement in her having been hit over the head and dumped in Fewston reservoir.

Even after she'd eventually been identified, I always had her in mind as the Woman in The Water. How she must have died at the hands of a supposed stranger never stopped haunting me. So how the hell is the elusive Tamara Fenton involved? The Tamara Fenton who we still haven't had the opportunity to speak to. Finding her has become even more of a priority.

47

MARTIN

IT'S NO GOOD. It all has to come out. I'll probably do time for how I disposed of Belinda's body but at least I've learned that I wasn't the one who killed her. I've spent six years believing it was all my fault but even now I know the truth, it doesn't make me feel any better about myself. I take a deep breath. Whatever happens, I'm just going to tell the truth. About *everything*. I don't see what else I can do. At least they won't arrest me straightaway. I've already been told I'll probably be admitted to a ward overnight for observation.

'If you could just start at the beginning.' DI Robinson settles himself into his seat as if he's getting comfy. 'How did you and Belinda come across Tamara and Dale Fenton? What was the initial connection between you all?'

'I hadn't heard of the Fentons until around six years ago when I returned home early from work,' I begin. 'I hadn't been feeling well so I'd been sent home early. When I saw an unfamiliar car outside, I sensed something was amiss.'

I'll never forget how my stomach lurched. It was the stuff of movies – husband arrives unexpectedly home from work to find his wife in bed with another man. 'Anyway, some bloke, who I later discovered was Dale, must have left through a door at the other side of the house and was scarpering to his car.' He clearly seemed to think he could get away without me seeing him.

'Did you know who he was at the time?'

'I had no idea. But my wife had become somewhat distant and I had started to suspect she might be up to something. It wasn't only that – she was doing all the other typical things as well – you know keeping her phone close, taking more care about her appearance, and she was really jumpy all the time.'

'Go on.'

'I had a bad taste in my mouth the moment I saw him. It was the speed at which he was leaving. He must have seen my headlights on the drive from one of the windows and fled from the house. I'd been married to Belinda for three years by then,' I tell him. Just the memory of her is making my head hurt even more. 'We'd been happy once, at least to start with.'

'And is home still that former farmhouse just outside Skipton?' He must be recalling the searches that were carried out after Belinda's body had been discovered.

I nod, the force of the movement hurting my head. 'I got back to find her racing around the bedroom, getting dressed as fast as she could. She'd thrown the covers back over the bed.'

'What did she tell you?'

'She tried lying of course – saying she was up there after having a nap. But she couldn't explain away the sock on the floor which I knew wasn't mine.' I swallow and wince again, not just with the physical pain but also with the mental pain of having to relive this story.

'I imagine that must have been a tough situation.'

It's the understatement of the century. 'I tried to walk away. I couldn't bear to look at her – I couldn't even bear to be in the same room as her.' I swallow. 'I felt sick, as you would when you discover your wife's carrying on with another man.'

I glance at the DI's left hand, his own wedding band gleaming from it. He's probably happily married. No doubt he'll never have endured anything close to the anguish I have over the last six years.

'Then what happened?'

'Belinda ran after me. She was screaming at me that it was all my fault, that I'd taken her for granted, that I never made any effort with our marriage. Then she told me she wanted me to move out – she and *Dale* as I then found out he was called, were going to be together. I was so angry – she was the one having the affair, yet she was ordering *me* to leave our home.' I lower my voice. If I don't, they'll be able to hear me in the adjacent cubicles. 'She wanted to make me homeless when I hadn't even done anything wrong.'

'Go on.'

'We were at the top of the stairs, and—' My voice falters.

'And?' The officer's head is tilted to one side like a dog waiting to be thrown a bone.

'I pushed her down them. I wanted her out of my way and in that awful moment, a cloud of red mist had come over me.' A memory of her face swims into my brain as she lost her balance. 'After what she'd done to me, I needed her as far away from me as possible.'

'Did Belinda fall right from the top to the bottom?' His voice is extremely calm given the extent of the lies I told the police at the time, in my initial statement, in interview, and to the press.

'No, only down the first set but she was really still. I didn't know whether she'd really hit her head or whether she was just pretending to be unconscious to punish me.' Both officers are watching me intently as they wait for me to continue. Beyond the cubicle I've been left in, life in accident and emergency continues. Buzzers, trolleys being wheeled past, barked instructions and pained voices. People will be in as much physical pain as I am but I doubt anyone's in as much mental pain.

'I panicked then,' I continue. 'I should have called for help or at the very least, I should have made sure Belinda was alright but instead, I just grabbed my keys and fled from the house. I needed to escape from what I'd done to her. I've never felt panic like it. I'd never laid a hand on a woman before and all I knew in that moment, was I'd pushed my wife, possibly to her death.'

DI Robinson nods along as I speak. 'Before we go any further, can you tell us how Tamara Fenton was involved in all this? You said before that *she'd* killed your wife.'

I take a deep breath. 'I only know now that Belinda wasn't dead when I left her.'

'But how can you say *Tamara Fenton* was somehow responsible?'

'As I left the house, there was another car, one I didn't recognise, parked up by one of the outbuildings. I don't know this for certain but I reckon now that it could have been Tamara, spying on her husband. I didn't do anything at the time, I was in too much of a state after what I'd done. So I just kept driving.'

'What you *thought* you'd done, you mean?'

'Yes. And knowing what I know now, I can look back and say that must have been the moment when Tamara went in.'

48

TAMARA

'Someone at the cottage is dead.' My sister appears in the kitchen doorway. 'Wayne went there after we'd left, looking for me.'

I continue making the tea. Such a normal activity. Such an abnormal day. Everything's changed – *everything*. And I'd give all I've got for it to be yesterday again.

'Did you hear me, Tamara? I said—'

'Yes, I heard you.'

The downstairs toilet flushes and Dale hurtles along the hallway. 'Did I just hear you right? Oh my God.'

'Which one?' I spoon sugar into Dale's mug, my hand surprisingly steady to say I've just found out I've killed again. I've been making Dale's drinks for so long, I know exactly how he likes them. A good domed teaspoon of sugar and his milk in first. Personally I can't understand that – I could never put the milk in first with my tea.

'Look at me, Tamara.' My sister's voice is more urgent. 'What's the matter with you?' She sounds as though she'd like to shake me. 'God knows what the boys might have seen. He had them in the back of the car.'

'I'm just making the tea.'

She marches over and spins me around to face her. 'Do you realise the shit that's going to hit us all now?' There are tears in her eyes. 'I've got the boys to think about.'

'Lucky you. At least you got to be a mother.' Tears fill my eyes too. For the baby that's bleeding away from me, for the mother I let down so badly and for the mother I'll never get to be. For one fleeting moment when I stared at that blob on the scan monitor, when I watched that heart beating as steadily as my own, I allowed myself to relax. Stupid me.

'I mean it, Tamara. This is going to affect them as well.'

'Nobody's being *forced* to have anything to do with this. It's *my* problem. So, I'll drink this tea, then I'll leave with Dale, and before long it will all blow over for the rest of you.'

'It's not a speeding fine, sis. You've *killed* someone.'

'Which one of them? Who?' Dale bursts into the kitchen.

Trust Dale to be so interested. If it's *her*, perhaps he'll be gutted that he's back to me being his only option. That's if we manage to get through this. Somehow, I doubt it.

I'm not going to tell my husband and sister that I meant to kill *both* Rachel *and* Martin. That I haven't succeeded could cause serious problems. Especially if it's Rachel I've killed and not Martin. If it's *him* who survives, he's bound to repeat what he now knows about me. So I need to find out what state whichever of them is in. Then I must find out where they are. This needs finishing properly.

I glare at Dale. 'All you care about is whether your slag of a girlfriend is alright.' I slam his mug down on the counter beside him, tea slopping all over the place as I storm from the kitchen. I need to be on my own. How can I go anywhere with Dale after what he's done to me? No, I think I know what I'm going to do. I'll take enough money to get me out of the country and I'll start again. On my own.

49

TAMARA

'WHAT DID you mean when you said you'd got away with it before?' My sister perches at the edge of the bed in her spare room beside me. I've stayed in this room many times over the years. I've always felt safe here, close to my sister and among the only family I've got now – my nephews. The most heart-breaking thing about being sent to prison after what I've done would be being kept apart from them as they continue to grow up. I can't imagine Ali and Wayne would ever allow them to visit a prison. And after the time I've spent as a visitor, I wouldn't want them to be there either.

'Where are Wayne and the boys?' I need to change the subject. 'You can't let them see me like this.'

'Never mind that right now.' Of course Ali isn't going to let this go. 'You said you'd done the same thing to Rachel as something you'd done before. I need to know what you were talking about.'

'I was just angry,' I reply. I can't look at her. If I do, I risk it all tumbling out. *All* of it. 'I just said it, alright?' Me and my big mouth. As if things aren't horrendous enough for me already, I've allowed adrenaline and misery to overcome me. I've let it all bubble up to the surface – memories that should have been well and truly buried. 'I was tired and stressed and then the bleeding sent me over the edge.'

'Oh come on, Tamara, I know you better than that.' She rests her hand on my arm. 'Out with it. Look, whatever it is, you know you can trust me.'

'I just don't want you to hate me.' A tear plops on the leg of the leggings she's lent me. I didn't even realise I was crying. 'It's really bad.' OK, I'm doing this. I'm actually going to tell her. Perhaps unburdening myself will somehow absolve me for the rest of it too.

'I could *never* hate you.' She pulls me closer and my tears fall faster. 'I'm your sister, for God's sake. We've been through thick and thin together.'

'But *you've* turned out alright, haven't you?' I wipe at my face with my hand. I'm sick of crying – I've had a lifetime of it. 'Despite everything we went through with Mum and Dad, you found happiness so it's not as if I can keep blaming our child-hood for how my life's turned out.'

'No matter what's happened or what you have or haven't done,' – she leans towards the bedside table, drags a tissue from the box and passes it to me. 'I just want to help you.'

'What's Dale doing now? He's still here, isn't he?' I dab at my eyes. Without him, I can't get away. No matter how much I'd like to leave on my own, I left the cottage without my bag so I've no access to our money.

'I've told him to wait downstairs and let us speak for a few minutes. The police could turn up at any time now that Wayne's given them our address. And *he* could be back with the boys at any moment too.'

I stare at the pattern on her carpet. I should have been staying in this room tonight, after taking care of my nephews. I should still have my baby growing inside me. Instead, my whole life's gone to shit. I don't know who to pin the blame on for it the most, Dale, Martin or Rachel.

'I'll definitely go to prison, won't I?' The reality of what I've done is only just starting to hit me. I thought I didn't care but now I'm away from that cottage and back in what almost feels like normality, I'm realising that I don't want to be locked up – I *can't* be locked up. I don't think my mind is strong enough to stand it.

'I really don't know, sis. But we'll find you a good solicitor. And I guess you've got mitigating circumstances.' She makes it sound so simple. 'But I still need to know what you meant when you said you'd got away with it before.'

The expression on Martin's face when I confessed what I'd done to Belinda slams back into my brain. Nobody knew a thing. And if it's *Martin* that's dead, no one else *ever* needs to know.

Ali clearly senses my continued hesitation. 'Come on, Tamara –you've alluded to this past event in front of both me *and* Dale. On some level, that means you need to talk about whatever it is.'

'I really don't.' I wrap my arms around myself as I rock back and forth on the comfy single bed. All I want to do is crawl under the duvet and sleep for the next twenty-four hours. I've had enough – I've truly had enough.

'Just tell me, Tamara. It can't be much worse than what's happened already.'

'Can't it?

'Just tell me.'

'But I've lived with it for so long already. And I'd managed to bury it before all this happened.'

'Lived with *what*? Buried *what*?' She's beginning to sound impatient.

'Do you *promise* I can trust you?' I look up at the face I've known since the day I was born. In our games as children, Ali was the mum and I was the child. She promised me she'd always look after me, no matter what. It's time to find out if she really meant that.

'How long have you known me?'

'OK, I'm going to tell you.' I swallow. 'It was six years ago,' I begin. I can hardly believe I'm going to finally tell her the truth. But she hasn't disowned me so far after what's already happened, so I'm as certain as I can be that she'll be able to handle this. Surely she'll understand. 'When I'd found out that Dale was having an affair. I'd been following him, watching him. And as you might imagine, I was gutted.'

'I can't believe you're still with him.' She shakes her head. 'How many times are you going to let him cheat on you? You deserve so much better.'

'None of that matters anymore.'

It's true. I'm probably going to be stuck in a prison cell before long. Like mother, like daughter. Has what I've done been worth it? Probably not. But it was cathartic in the moment.

'I'd followed Dale to some farmhouse at the edge of Skipton, which I now know was Martin's house,' I continue.

'Martin's?' My sister's voice is almost a screech.

'Just listen. Anyway, I parked up at the edge of the track and turned my lights off. His wife didn't even bother to close the curtains. I watched them take each other's clothes off in the lounge.' The memory of my husband standing there with no clothes on in front of Belinda Sanders is a memory I wish I could lose. And to think he's done this with two more women since then. Two more that I know of anyway. 'And then a light went on in an upstairs room. It was agony. I wanted to storm in there, to demand he stop and come home with me but I was paralysed. I just couldn't believe what he was doing to me.'

'Oh Tamara.' Ali reaches for my hand. 'You need to sort this out. You need to talk to someone. Something inside you is telling you this is all you deserve. But it's not true.'

'Like I said, none of that matters anymore.' At any moment there'll be a huge banging at Ali's door. I might have washed all the blood from myself, and my clothes might be going round and round in Ali's washing machine but if I haven't got away before the police arrive, I'm certain they'll take one look at me and see the blood on my hands. Whether I've washed it away or not.

'I *tried* not to watch,' I say, the memory making me feel sicker than I already do. 'Then afterwards, they came back downstairs and were in the kitchen together, hugging, kissing and—' My voice trails off. I've loved Dale since the moment I clapped eyes on him as a teenager. Him being so geeky back then and my broken home made us both targets for the bullies. We promised that we'd always be there for the other. And then it became more than that. Within a year, he vowed that one day, he'd give me the home and stable family life I'd never known. Obviously babies were supposed to be a part of that. The babies that I don't seem to be able to hang onto.

'While I was parked there, another car came up behind me on the track. I had to duck down to make sure the driver didn't see me. Thankfully, it went straight past and parked up.'

'I watched Dale run around from what must have been an entrance at the other side of their house.' I look into my sister's face. She's listening intently.

'Then what happened?'

'Dale jumped into his car and scarpered.' I was still watching at a distance with my lights off. He didn't even notice me as he screeched past. He'd have been more focused on getting away from Martin, who'd clearly come home early.

'Did you hang around?'

'I got out of the car and crept towards the house. Belinda and Martin sounded like they were upstairs. They were shouting – of course they were. He'd not exactly caught her in the act but he was pretty close. It didn't take a genius to work out what was going on.' I recall the sympathy I felt towards the man in that moment. I knew how he must be feeling. After all, I knew how I was feeling. 'That went on for a few minutes then there were a couple of loud bangs, followed by a scream. Then he came hurtling back through the door he'd arrived by and jumped back into his car. I assumed he must be going after Dale.'

I'll never forget how empty I felt. Dale was probably heading back home to me, ready to act like nothing had happened – just as he'd been doing for several months.

However, I had to act. Now I knew the truth, I *had* to do *something.*

50

ALI

'WHAT ARE YOU DOING UP THERE?' Dale's voice is edged with impatience as it echoes up the stairs.

I march to the door and poke my head around it. 'Leave us be for a bit longer please. I'm talking to Tamara.'

'I've got a right to be part of your conversation.' He starts up the stairs. 'I need to know what she's telling you.'

'You can wait, Dale.' I march to the top of the stairs, blocking his way. 'She's talking to *me* for a few minutes. You're lucky I've even let you inside my house after how you've treated her. This is *your* fault, all of it is. Do you hear me?'

'You do realise that while you're having your cosy chat, the police could turn up at any time?'

'Of course I do, and we won't be much longer.'

She's so close to telling me something which sounds like it's going to be colossal that we need to continue.

By some miracle, Dale turns on his heel and heads back downstairs. I return to my sister who's leaning forward on the bed, her head in her hands.

'I'm here for you sis.' I reach for her hand. 'I'm always here for you – I'm not going anywhere.'

'No, but I probably am.' She raises her face to look at me. 'If Martin's survived the belt I gave him with the poker, the first thing he'll do is tell the police what he's discovered about me.'

'So tell me what happened next – after Martin had driven away.' I steel myself for what must be coming. I already have a very good idea.

'She and Martin must have come to blows before I went in there,' she continues. 'She seemed a bit dazed to start with, asking me who I was and how I'd got in. She also had blood running down the side of her head.'

'So, presumably he'd attacked her? After finding her with Dale?' My brother-in-law has so much to answer for. Why get married if one woman isn't enough? Has he any idea just how much hurt and destruction his behaviour causes?

'It looked like he had. Anyway I told her who I was and to start with, I was begging her to stay away from him.' Tears are coursing down her cheeks. 'I told her I'd been with him since we were at school and pleaded with her to leave him alone. I loved him, Ali. And despite everything, I still do.'

'I know you do.' I rub at the top of her hand. 'Though God knows why.'

'She said things had already gone too far for that. She was crying too as she told me she was pregnant with Dale's baby and that he was planning to leave me, and that she was planning to leave her husband.' Her words are tumbling out. 'She said she was sorry to hurt me and her husband but that she and Dale were going to have the baby, and they were going to be a family.'

'Oh, sis.' I sit closer to her and put my arm around her shoulders. She's shaking as the sobs rack her body.

'It had been three days since I'd had a miscarriage.' Tamara can barely get her words out. 'There was only one thing I was going to do to Belinda Sanders.'

'What do you mean?'

'I think I went into some kind of trance. I'm not even sure I knew what I was doing. Well, maybe I did, I just don't know. She told me to leave but instead, I lunged for one of the tools hanging in the fireplace. A fire poker just like I used back at the cottage.'

'And you belted her with it?'

She nods. 'I didn't give her a chance to fight back. I just whacked her as hard as I could. I got her at the side of her head and she fell down onto her knees straight away. I wiped the poker clean and ran off. Once seems to have been all it took.'

'Ali, are you up there?' It takes a moment or two for me to come to my senses. Wayne's home.

'We need to act normal in front of the boys,' I say. 'Somehow. They can't know about any of this – they're far too little.'

She blows her nose and stands from the bed, nodding.

'No, you wait up here,' I say. 'Get yourself back together. I need to tell Wayne what's going on. And I think you and Dale should stay apart for the moment. I'll tell him you need a few more minutes. He shouldn't know any of this. Not yet, anyway.'

'Please don't say anything to Wayne either. Not the *full* story.'

I don't reply as I close the door. I don't keep secrets from my husband, especially secrets on this scale.

'We need to get the police here *now*.' Wayne hisses as I finish telling him what Tamara's just confessed to. 'She's belted *three* people with a solid metal rod, killing at least two of them and she's now up there in our spare room.'

'She's still my sister,' I reply.

'This is all beyond us, love.' He reaches for my hand. 'We're out of our depth. And it's this sort of thing you wanted to turn your back on, remember – all the drama, all the misery?'

'It's an absolute nightmare.' I dab at my eyes. 'And I don't know what to do. Of course the police will need to know, but I don't want to be the one—'

'I want to know what's going on.' Dale bangs on the door of the kitchen. 'I've got a right to know. I've waited long enough now.'

I tug it open. 'I've asked you to stay in there with the boys. Please, Dale, just do this one thing for me while I'm talking to Wayne. I'll speak to you in five minutes.' I slam the door after him.

'You should have dropped the kids off with your dad.' I retake my seat on the breakfast bar stool, eyeing up the brandy on top of the fridge. I could be forgiven for pouring myself a triple but I'd better wait until I know what's going to happen. When the police turn up, all hell's going to break loose. Tamara could still run for it, but I've cooled on that idea now that I'm back in my reality. I don't want to lie or cover for her. I'll probably be in enough trouble as it is for letting her shower here and for washing her clothes.

'They're both on their screens. And we're not shouting or anything. It's fine.'

'It won't be fine when the police get here.'

'But they're going to realise sooner or later that something's going on.' His voice starts to rise. 'When they don't see their auntie for a few years, for instance.'

'I thought you said no one's shouting.'

'I'm sorry – it's just – God, Ali, I saw them carting the body bag out of there – I even thought it was *you*.' He looks me straight in the eye. 'What the hell have we managed to get mixed up in?'

51

MARTIN

'ARE YOU NEARLY DONE IN HERE?' The same nurse as before pokes her head into the cubicle. 'A bed's become available so we'll be getting ready to move you shortly.'

'Are you OK to keep going?' DI Robinson doesn't look at the nurse but keeps his attention on me.

I nod. I'm not OK but I have to keep going. I'm already maxed out with painkillers and dread to think what the pain would be like without them. I must have a skull of steel though. They've glued the gash she caused for now but I might still need stitches. 'I'm OK. Can I just have a glass of water, please?' My mouth's dry. It's probably the absolute anxiety of what I'm about to tell them. But I've lived with it for so long, it's time for it to come out into the open. All of it.

'We can take a break at any time.' He pours some water into my beaker from the jug at the edge of the cubicle. 'Just say the word.'

'I'll come back in twenty minutes then.' The nurse pulls the curtain back across and her footsteps die away.

'Thanks.' I take the water from him. 'I'd rather get this over and done with.'

At least then, they might be able to tell me what I'm likely to be facing. Perhaps they'll be more lenient since I'm *confessing* to what I did, but even I know it's six years too late.

'OK, we'll continue.' DI Robinson drops back into his seat as I gulp from my glass, the movement hurting my head even more. 'So, after the row, after you'd pushed your wife down the stairs and left the house, where did you go?'

'I was just driving around and around in a blind panic. Really I wanted to go to the pub, to drink myself into oblivion but deep down, I *knew* I might have hurt her when I pushed her. And I'm really not that kind of man, despite what you might be thinking of me.'

Neither of the officers say anything but I'm certain they exchange glances. But how could they know of the rage that took hold of me when I discovered Belinda's affair. It was so visceral, I could taste it.

'As soon as I started to calm down, I knew I'd have to go back to make sure she was alright. To apologise for hurting her. What she'd done to me was terrible, but pushing her like that felt even worse.' I don't add that I just did nearly the same thing again when I pushed Tamara into the cellar. One story at a time is bad enough. Besides, I'm sure she'll be telling her side of the tale by now. Perhaps she'll get off with belting us both with that poker after what we did to her.

'So you went back?'

I take a deep breath. The sight of my wife bent double, face down on the floor is a vision that's never left me, even six years on. It's little wonder that I went to pieces when looking at Rachel slumped in exactly the same way. 'She was dead when I walked in.' Tears fill my eyes as I recall how I even slapped her face to try and wake her. I'll leave that part out here though. 'I didn't think she'd hit her head that hard when I pushed her and I left, but I've lived for all this time thinking I must have been mistaken. I was convinced she'd only fallen halfway down the stairs, but in my state of mind at the time, I couldn't be sure. Even if she had managed to stand and had fallen again while I was out, I was still convinced I was responsible for her death.'

'So you're definitely saying you *weren't*?'

'Like I said, the man who'd fled from my house was Dale,' I reply. 'But Tamara was there as well. And *she* killed my wife.' A tear rolls from my face and plops onto the sheet that's covering me. I watch as the moisture spreads through the fabric. 'She admitted it – right after she attacked Rachel at the cottage, just before she turned the poker onto me and left me for dead. She obviously didn't expect me to be able to repeat what she'd confessed to.'

52

DI ROBINSON

THE PLOT THICKENS. My own head's starting to buzz with keeping all this together. I glance across at my colleague, his expression passive as he continues to scribble the notes we'll shortly have to act on.

'So you're saying Tamara Fenton *confessed* to killing Belinda, your wife?'

He nods. 'But in the belief *I'd* killed her, it was *me* who moved her body from the house.'

'We did a thorough search of your home and didn't find anything to suggest what had happened there.'

'I'd had two months to bleach and clean every square inch of it before you found her body.' He stares down at the hands that will have done all the cleaning. Hands that will have weighted down Belinda Sander's body and disposed of it like a piece of rubbish.

'Why would you get rid of her like you did if someone else had killed her?'

'At the time, I really thought it was me. I'd pushed her, hadn't I?'

I'll never forget the interviews I had with this man. He was absolutely distraught throughout the investigation. He barely kept it together during the press conferences while we searched for her. Even the *it's always the husband* brigade was silent on social media. Everyone seemed to be rooting for Martin. Me included. Of course we questioned him and searched both his car and his home, but two months on, we didn't find a scrap of evidence.

'So it was *you* who actually dumped her body in the reservoir?'

'I was terrified of going to prison.'

'You do realise that as soon as you've been given medical clearance we're going to have to arrest you?' My tone is far sharper now I know I'm dealing with a criminal rather than a victim.

'Of course.' He closes his eyes.

'Now if you could answer the question please.'

'Yes, it was me. But I wasn't alone.'

'Oh?'

'Dale Fenton came back.'

This just gets worse. After hearing all this, I'll be more glad than ever to get home to my own wife and kids this evening. When I see the darkness that exists between people who are supposed to love one another, at times, I can barely believe it. I'm filled with gratitude that I get to clock off from this world each day and can return to my normal life. 'But you'd said he'd already run out and driven off.'

'He said Belinda had called him and told him I'd pushed her. So *he* believed I'd killed her too when he walked in.'

I cast my mind back. We *must* have checked all the call logs at the time. And Dale must have given a plausible reason as to why Belinda had called his number when he was contacted by us. I'm going to have to check this out or our heads could be rolling if something's been missed. Or perhaps she called him through an encrypted service like WhatsApp.

'So at no time during this initial aftermath, did you think of seeking help from us?'

He shakes his head. 'To be honest, I wasn't thinking straight. All I could think about was getting Belinda out of the house. All I could focus on was getting rid of her body.'

'How did Dale react when he arrived?'

'He was distraught. To begin with, he kept saying over and over again, *what have you done? What have you done to them?* That was how I discovered she'd been pregnant.' His voice wobbles. 'It was a horrendous shock.'

'I imagine finding Belinda dead like that was a shock for Dale as well.'

'We probably should have been knocking ten bells out of each other but it just didn't happen.'

'So what *did* happen?'

'I offered Dale two options.'

He's so calm as he regales his story to us, which is concerning in itself, though I suppose he's had six years to compose this. That he was also calm enough to offer his wife's lover 'options' in the wake of finding his wife's body suggests something else entirely. 'And what were these *options*?'

'The first was that Dale could report what he'd just walked in on and be dragged into it all. He *would* have been a suspect. I saw he was wearing a wedding ring, so I told him that his wife would discover what he'd been up to and his marriage would also be over.'

'And what was the other option?' This is where it gets interesting. I glance over the bed at Sergeant Bennett to make sure he's still on high alert and noting everything down. These pocket notes will be more than enough to arrest Tamara Fenton and once we've got her on tape, bringing charges should be a doddle.

'I suggested he could help me. If he did, I'd keep him completely out of things, whatever happened.'

'Help you? How?' Like I really need to ask. I'm pretty sure I know what's coming.

'Are you still here?' The nurse is back. She's certainly a battleaxe. 'Martin needs to rest. It's Doctor's orders now. You'll have to come back tomorrow.'

'No, honestly, I'm OK. We're nearly done.' On some level, this will go in his favour. It might have come six years too late but at least he's finally willing to tell us the whole story. Once we know exactly what Dale Fenton did to *help*, we'll know which grounds we're arresting him on too.

'Just a few more minutes. But then we really must take Martin up to the ward.'

'It was late in the evening.' Martin's face clouds over. Remembering must be causing him even more pain than he's already in. 'We wrapped Belinda in some waterproof sheeting I had in the garage and between us, we got her into the boot.'

'We went on the B roads to avoid any cameras,' he says. 'And we drove her to Fewston.' This figures. It's pitch dark there at night. People only ever walk around the water during daylight hours.

'Tell me *exactly* what you did next.'

53

DI ROBINSON

'WE DROVE to the beachy bit where the picnic tables are and placed some small rocks inside her clothing to weigh her down.' He hangs his head.

The shadow of this woman and her unborn baby has never left me. She was around eight week's pregnant, and at the time, we assumed the baby was her husband's and two of our more specially trained officers went to inform him. They'd reported back, saying his reaction had been one of shock and that he'd asked them to leave, saying he needed to be alone.

'You've no idea how sorry I am. I'd do anything to turn back the clock.'

So would I. For all these years, the Belinda Sanders case has remained open. The only conclusion we could draw at the time was she must have been randomly attacked on the footpath which runs around the reservoir. In the aftermath, two other women had come forward, both saying they'd been followed and felt threatened, which strengthened our theory. Reports, as it's turning out, that were nothing more than a coincidence.

'So you and Dale Fenton just carried on with your normal lives?' And families continued to enjoy their picnics at the side of the reservoir, not realising a weighted-down body was residing just metres from them.

'No, I didn't, not really.' He points at a box of tissues next to the jug of water which Sergeant Bennett passes to him. Martin blows his nose and seems to wince at the pain it's causing him. Good. He deserves every bit of it. We won't be able to do him for murder, but we'll be able to do him for perverting the course of justice and unlawful disposal of a body. The same goes for Dale Fenton. 'Life was never going to go back to normal after that, was it?'

'Go on.'

'Dale and I had agreed never to contact each other again. But to be honest, I couldn't let him go.'

'What do you mean?'

'While we were sorting the situation with Belinda out, I'd taken a look inside his car. There was a parcel on his passenger seat so I had his full name and address.'

'What did you want that for?'

'Just in case.' He takes a deep breath. 'I tried to just go on, but as the months passed, I have to admit that I became completely obsessed with the man who'd been sleeping with my wife. The one who must have got her pregnant. I knew it wasn't *my* baby – that side of our marriage had dried up, which was another reason I'd suspected her of having an affair.'

'I imagine her pregnancy must have been really hard for you to deal with.' A little sympathy should keep him talking. I glance at my watch. The department has quietened somewhat since we first arrived. I've lost track of how long we've been talking to Martin Sanders but it's far longer than it should have been. But we've just about got all we need.

'*Hard* is putting it mildly. If I'm honest, I couldn't let it go. I couldn't let *him* go. Not just because of who he was and what he'd done to my marriage, but also because he was harbouring the secret that could blow my life to bits if he ever spoke up.'

'But he'd have blown his own life to bits as well if he'd spoken up, wouldn't he?'

'At the time, I honestly thought it was *me* who'd killed Belinda. Anyway, I wanted to know *everything* I could about him. Where he worked, where he lived, who he lived with...' His voice trails off. 'And then I saw him with Tamara.'

'Was that the first time you'd seen her in person?'

He nods. 'I'd already seen pictures of her on Facebook and couldn't believe how like Belinda she was. Then when I saw her in the flesh, I felt a weird sort of connection.'

'Because your wife and her husband had been having an affair?'

'I guess so. We'd both been treated the same by them and yet, as far as I could tell, she had no idea what her husband had been up to or what he was capable of.' He takes a deep breath. 'He'd helped me dispose of Belinda's body, then seemed to be going about his life as if nothing had ever happened. So I felt quite protective towards Tamara.'

'Really?'

'Before long, I became more fixated on her than Dale. It probably wasn't helpful that she really is the absolute spitting image of Belinda. Their appearance, their mannerisms, even the way they speak.'

I want to correct the word *speak* to *spoke* as he refers to his dead wife. After all, her voice is now silenced forever.

'I'll admit I fell in love with Tamara.'

'But you didn't even know her, did you?'

'I watched her for years. I *did* know her. I also knew I could give her a better life than *he* could. But that's all gone now – now that I know what she's done.'

'We attended the Fenton's house on Wednesday evening, Sir.' My sergeant's voice is croaky after being silent while he's been scribbling notes down for so long. 'To investigate reports of a man hanging around. And not for the first time, I might add – far from it.'

Martin stays silent.

'I take it you'd be the man?'

He looks down at his thumbs as he twirls them around and around each other. 'Yes.'

'So tell me, given that she'd made a complaint about you, how did you and Tamara come to be at a cottage in the Yorkshire Dales together. You, her, and her neighbour, Rachel?'

'It was Rachel who helped set everything up. She said Tamara felt the same about me. But she lied.'

'Oh and also to clarify – would you be the *M*' – he draws quotes in the air, – 'who the card and the roses were from on Rachel's lounge windowsill which we found when checking her property?'

He nods. 'They were meant as a thank you – for bringing me and Tamara together.'

'And what can you tell me about a Ford S-Max, registration Yankee, Delta, One, Seven, Lima, Yankee, Delta?'

'I was going to go back for it. I hid it in the hedge. It was only supposed to be there for one night.'

'You hid it in the hedge?'

'If Tamara had seen it outside the cottage, she wouldn't have come in. She thought I was Dale to start with. That he'd planned a surprise for her.'

I stare back at him. 'I think we've got enough from you for now, Martin. But we'll be back tomorrow and clearly things won't be quite so comfortable for you then.' I nod at his trolley.

'In fact,' I say to Sergeant Bennet as we exit the hospital. 'We need to ensure things for Martin Sanders are as uncomfortable as we can possibly make them.'

EPILOGUE
ALI – 7 MONTHS LATER

I HAVEN'T TOLD anyone where I'm going today. Not even Wayne. He doesn't understand the bond I have with my sister, even after what she pleaded guilty to. What he's failing to grasp is that even after what she's done, she's still a victim of it all. She's a victim of our parents, a victim of Dale's awful treatment of her and a victim of her fear of being alone. Plus, in both instances of her violence, she was maddened with grief after miscarriages and no doubt all the hormones that went along with that.

There's a jovial atmosphere in the visitors' centre as people check in. As if they're at an airport. I'm surprised at how many children are here – all looking smart and expectant. Dressed in what are, no doubt, their best clothes for their fortnightly trip to visit their mothers. The poor kids. I don't know how anyone can bring their children to a place like this. I couldn't.

It's certainly airport-style security as I reach the second building, the one that's in between the visitor's centre and the main hall. Only the checks are far more stringent than at an airport. I'm photographed, fingerprinted, searched, scanned and finally, they look in my mouth and down my top. I couldn't feel any less dignified as I reach the final seating area. When I get to the other side of that door, I'll get to see my sister for the first time since her sentencing.

They tried to slap her with murder charges to begin with. But they couldn't make those stick and they were swiftly downgraded to manslaughter on the grounds of diminished responsibility for what she's done to Rachel and Belinda. She also pleaded guilty to causing grievous bodily harm to Martin, but again, on the grounds of diminished responsibility.

I've never felt as low as I did when she was taken down, sobbing. She looked back at me before being led through the final door and all I saw were our mother's eyes.

Wayne seems to think I can put it all behind me and just get on with my life but I can't. Nothing could have prepared me for the turmoil I've been through since Valentine's Day.

'Rowlings, Parker, Smith, Browne, Fenton.' I hate how my sister is referred to by her surname only. *Her name's Tamara, and she's a person. She's my sister.* I want to tell them straight but if I were to challenge any of these hard-faced officers, I'd probably be turned away at this final hurdle.

'Tamara Fenton,' I announce when I arrive at the desk.

'Table seven.' The female officer points across the room without even looking at me. 'If we could just have your fingerprint again please.'

I thread my way through the happy conversations to the table where I must wait for my sister. Inmates are being let out of a door in the corner of the visiting room one at a time. I watch as each face lights up as they spot their loved ones. It won't be the same in two hours though – at the end of their visit when they're forced to part company. I'm dreading leaving

Tamara in this place. Seeing her here will be hard enough. Leaving her here will be even harder.

She's the last one through the door. Looking pale and skinny, she approaches my table. 'We're only allowed to give brief hugs,' she mutters. 'Or else we get searched afterwards.'

I can only imagine what that entails, so I briefly draw her bony shoulders towards me, getting a whiff of cheap shampoo from her thinning hair before quickly letting her go again.

'I could murder a cuppa,' she says. It's good to see her smile. It's a long time since I've seen it.

'Coming right up. I might as well get to the counter now while there's no queue. Then we can talk.'

'Sounds ominous.' She forces a laugh even though we both know the worst is over. She just needs to serve her time, get parole and then get out to rebuild her life.

A vision of my mother fills my mind as I wait for our drinks to be made. Talk about history repeating itself. The irony of where I am is plaguing me even more now that I'm here. I never visited my mother when she was locked up – even when I was told she was down to her final weeks of life. I suspected I might regret it, but I couldn't bring myself to see her again. The whole situation had dragged me to the floor, and for my sanity, I'd said enough was enough.

However, Tamara always visited. When Mum was transferred to a secure hospital ward to see out her last days, Tamara spent as much time as she was allowed at her bedside. I just buried what was happening and vowed to do something different to the toxicity I'd always known. To have my own happy family and to make something of my life.

And I have.

The women behind the counter are as drawn and thin as my sister. What a place to end up. I ask for chocolate and crisps to be added to my tray and pay for it with my debit card, the only item I've been allowed to bring into the visiting room. I feel strange not putting it back into my purse and it's odd not to have my handbag on my shoulder. I just hope the lockers where we've been made to leave all our possessions are secure.

Tamara's watching me as I return to our table, no doubt savouring her first point of contact with the outside world since she found out she'd be stuck here for at least eleven years. She'd be a mother by now if none of it had happened. I'd be an auntie. If Dale could have just kept it in his trousers and looked after his wife instead of cheating on her. Instead she's been left to rot in here, with me as her only visitor.

I transfer all the items from the tray to the table which I then rest at the side of my seat.

'It's like the days when we used to have midnight feasts, isn't it?' She opens the spout in the lid of her polystyrene cup. 'I'm ready for this. It feels like I've been waiting in that holding room forever.'

'Don't remind me.' The midnight feasts are one of our happier memories of childhood. All my happy childhood memories involve my sister. When it was me and her against our parents, our bullies and everything else that befell us as children. After years of stuffing it down, the past has come back with a bang. And after everything that's happened, I can't seem to push it down again. Wayne wants me to go for more counselling but I'm too scared about what else it might open up. 'So how are you doing in here?'

'I'm OK.' She pulls a packet of crisps apart. 'It's easier than I thought it would be, especially now I've been sentenced.'

'Really?' I look around the yellow walls with a shudder. 'I thought it would be worse, *knowing* how long you've got to serve.'

'I can just put my head down and get on with it, can't I?'

'And how are you doing that?' I'm certain I'd go stir crazy if locked in a place like this.

'There's work, education, the gym, reading, honestly, I'm alright.' Her voice is bright, but *too* bright.

'What about the other women?' I glance around the room again. Everyone's deep in conversation. But an inmate two tables to my right is in tears. And so is her little girl. I can't imagine what it must be like to only see your children for two hours, once a fortnight. Whatever their circumstances, my heart goes out to them.

'They're OK mainly. I get on fine with my padmate and then when I'm let out at association, to be honest, the other women look up to me. What I've done earns you extra *points* in here.' She draws air quotes as she says the word points. It sounds odd to hear my sister use words like *padmate* and *association*. But after six months on remand, and a month since her sentencing, she's bound to have picked up the lingo.

'Have you heard anything from Dale since you were last in court?'

'He's written to me a couple of times but I've torn his letters up without reading them. I can't really understand why he'd want to be in touch with the woman who killed not only one, but *two* of his mistresses?' She laughs, but the sound is hollow. There's a different air about her. It's as if she no longer feels the same level of shame for what she's done. I suppose she won't if the other women are looking up to her for it.

'He's not exactly blameless is he? I can't believe he helped dump Belinda's body. You think you know someone...' Her voice trails off. 'At least he's had *some* punishment.'

'Not long enough if you ask me.' I can't keep the bitterness from my words.

'They got the same, didn't they? In terms of what they'll actually serve anyway?'

'It's wrong, all wrong,' I reply. 'Martin's sentence for stalking you and false imprisonment should have been *added* to what he got for dumping his wife's body, not ordered to be served concurrently.'

'At least he's been sent down,' she replies before laughing again. 'Wouldn't it be funny if they were in the same prison? Or the same *cell*. I hope they knock the shit out of each other.'

'I'm sure they'll be in different places,' I say. It makes my blood boil that they'll be out, back living their lives years before my sister can. I blame them both for how and where she's ended up. By the time she's free, she'll be in her late forties and that's only if she's granted parole the first time.

It baffles me how differently two people can act in response to the same thing. After disposing of Belinda's body, Dale continued in an untroubled way, whereas Martin has spent the last six years wracked with guilt.

Then there's the difference in how Tamara and Martin dealt with their spouse's infidelity. Martin lashed out at his wife, whereas Tamara went for the women Dale was unfaithful with, rather than *him*.

Then, of course, there's how my sister and I coped with our mother's incarceration after our father's death. I ran a mile from the situation, while Tamara stuck around and visited her in prison. One thing I do know is that she's coping far better in *this* place than I ever could. I really would go to pieces if I was locked up in here.

'How's the salon doing?' She asks, brightening some more. 'And the girls? Did you call in again like you said you would?'

'It's all ticking over nicely,' I reply. She doesn't need to know about the aggro I've had from Wayne for agreeing to oversee its management, or the job I had persuading Sian and Jae to stay there after the storm in the news and on social media. It erupted again for a couple of days straight after Tamara was sentenced but it's thankfully all died down again.

I wrack my brains for something else to say. We only spoke on the phone a couple of days ago so we exhausted most subjects we could have talked about now. My boys, the packing up of her house and what we've both been doing. It's difficult when all her days are much the same and she doesn't have a great deal of conversation to impart. It'll be like this until she becomes eligible for parole. Then, and only then, can she perhaps begin to plan for the future.

'At least I'm going to get out of here eventually.' It's as if she's read my mind. 'Unlike poor Mum.' It's also as if she knows that I was only thinking about Mum a few minutes ago. Being here must be bringing things back for her too.

'I thought Mum was a no-go topic of discussion.' I sip at my tea. It's vile but it's better than nothing. I'm thirsty after all the waiting around I've done to get in here.

'Maybe it's time to change that.' Her voice is quiet – in fact, it's barely perceptible beneath the din in here.

'What?' I'm beginning to wish I'd never come. The last person I want to discuss is our mother. But if it helps Tamara, I'll have to indulge her, if only for a few minutes.

'Mum should *never* have been in here.'

'We both know that.'

'It was all *his* fault – our bloody *father's*.' She spits the word out like it's something nasty in her mouth.

'Do we really have to talk about him?'

'Yes, we do.'

'It's *got* to be easier for you – your conscience is much clearer than mine as far as Mum was concerned. At least you visited her.' I look to the table next to us, imagining Tamara and Mum sitting facing each other, just like we are now. 'What did the two of you talk about anyway? You never told me.' I can't believe I'm going here with our conversation. I'm going to pay for it later, when I've left my sister and it's all swirling around in my brain. 'Was it all just smalltalk like we try to get away with on the phone, or did she ever try to address what she did to Dad?'

'He deserved everything he got.' She rests her crisp packet onto the table as if she can't face eating anymore. I don't blame her. It's not exactly an appetising subject to talk about your mother shoving a knife into your father's stomach. 'After all that misery he put her through. The beatings, the affairs, the misery he put us *all* through.'

'She could have just left him,' I reply. 'It was as if she'd settled for that kind of life. Maybe she felt she deserved nothing better. If she'd just left him, she could have started again. Instead of completely ruining her life and ending up in here.'

I cast my eyes around the visiting room, at its many cameras and prison officers staring in turn at everybody as if anything at any moment could happen. Perhaps it could.

'She stopped *me* from ruining *my* life actually.' Tamara fiddles with the edge of her cup, seeming to be avoiding my gaze.

'How do you mean?' She's never said anything like this before. Normally our conversations hinge on the damage our parents caused us and it's the first time we've allowed the subject of our Mum *killing* our Dad into our discussion.

'Mum didn't kill him.' She looks down at the floor.

'I don't understand.'

'He had her up against a wall. He was screaming into her face.' She still won't meet my eye.

'Are you saying it was *you*?' Oh my God. I had *no* idea this situation could get any worse.

'I rushed up behind him with the knife and when he swung around, I stuck it into his gut.'

It takes a moment before I can speak.

'Say something, Ali.'

I stare at her. 'I just can't believe it.'

'And Mum, well she—'

'You let her take the blame? You let her serve your time? How could you?' I feel sick. My poor mother.

'She wanted to protect me. She felt like her life was over anyway but said I had the whole of mine in front of me. She told me I needed to make every second count.'

I blink back my tears. 'And you've really done that haven't you?' I can't keep the sarcasm from my voice.

'Do you know something, sis?'

'What?' I can't believe she's calling me *sis* as though nothing's happened. It's as if she hasn't just admitted that she killed our father and let our mother take the blame.

'I'd do it all again, I would. To all of them. But this time, I'd hit Martin twice, three times – as many times as it took. He should be six foot under like the rest of them. None of this would have ever come out then.'

'I know what he did but—'

'They *all* deserved what they got. Especially our father.'

'Mum didn't deserve what she got though, did she?' I couldn't forgive myself *before* for never visiting her, even when she probably needed me the most at the end, so I've no chance of forgiving myself *now*.

I can't breathe. All the old feelings are coming back. I need to get out of here. I get to my feet.

'Ali.' My sister's voice sounds far away as I arrive at the desk I checked in at. 'Please don't go.'

A hush falls over the room. 'I need to leave,' I tell the officer sitting behind it. 'Please open the door.'

'Ali!' Tamara's anguished voice echoes behind me.

I don't look back at my sister as I leave the gloom of the visiting room. It's only when I've made it back through the seated area and out into the sunny afternoon that the tears start to fall. For the family we never were and how it's all turned out.

I won't visit again. I can't. Perhaps Tamara and I will see

each other again when she's eventually released, but maybe not. Right now, all that matters is distancing myself from the endless drama and returning home to my sons and Wayne.

Back to my family. Back to normal life. As I once said to Tamara, *life is for living, not just existing.* But for the foreseeable future, I will be taking the same stance over Valentine's Day as Dale – and forgetting it...

The End

Before you Go

Thank you for reading The Valentine – I hope you enjoyed it!

If you want more, check out I Don't Like Mondays on Amazon, my next psychological thriller, where you'll meet Cathy.

She's woken up in intensive care without any memory of her recent life or having narrowly cheated death.

With the help of her family, friends and witness testimonies, she must piece together who she really is and what led to the events of that Monday morning, when she found herself in the path of the 7.02 train to London King's Cross.

For a FREE novella, please Join my 'keep in touch' list where I can also keep you posted of special offers and new releases. You can join by visiting my website www.mariafrank land.co.uk.

BOOK CLUB DISCUSSION QUESTIONS

1. Discuss the effect their parents marriage and its consequences have had on Tamara and Ali into adulthood.

2. What is the hold Dale has had over Tamara for so many years?

3. Is there any justification for Tamara's actions?

4. *We women should stick together. Not go after each other's husbands.* Talk about what Ali said to Rachel. What motivates a woman to pursue a married man?

5. Discuss Martin's state of mind with regard to his fixation on Dale and then Tamara.

6. *Stalkers are encouraged to attack and threaten.* Discuss with reference to the reluctance by the police to intervene in a situation where no one has yet been physically threatened.

7. Try to imagine what Martin's Valentine's Day evening expectations might have been.

8. As alluded to in the story, do *you* think Valentine's Day is *a load of commercial nonsense*?

9. Talk about the differences between Ali and Tamara and how their lives have ended up.

10. What are your feelings about the twist right at the end of the story? Discuss why Tamara and Ali's mother carried the blame and took a prison sentence her daughter should have served.

11. What should Ali do now – now that she knows the truth about her mother?

12. How might life look for each of the characters in the aftermath of this story?

I DON'T LIKE MONDAYS – PROLOGUE

I pull into the station car park, unable to recall the journey after the speakerphone argument that's endured since I left the house. My hands tremble on the steering wheel as I glance into the rearview mirror. Dishevelled hair and the shadows beneath my eyes are darker than ever. Insomnia has marked me, and it shows. I rummage in my handbag, searching for my hairbrush and compact. Some quick fixes are essential – I can't face the pre-interview presentation looking like this.

Dragging my wheelie case from the boot, I sigh, breathing clouds of breath into the freezing air. *It's as though you can't wait to get away from us.* It's not the argument I've just had that's needling me the most, more what my husband said as I searched for my keys. His words play on a loop in my mind, as relentless as the rumble of passing trains.

My cheeks burn with sudden warmth inside the station, and my stomach growls as the scent of coffee and warm crois-sants hits me. I check my watch – I have ten minutes to spare so there's enough time to grab something. Food might settle the growing unease in my gut.

As I wait at the counter for my order, my phone vibrates in

my coat pocket with a message. For a moment, I hardly dare to look at it. Is it a friend or a foe?

> Stay away from him, do you hear me? Just bloody stay away.

It's swiftly followed by another one. At first, I think it's *her* again but no, it's a different sender. It seems that everyone's out to get me this morning.

> May the best woman win. And just for the record, it won't be you. Good luck Cathy – you're going to need it.

The words sting, as sharp and biting as the frost outside. Tears well up, blurring my vision. This Monday morning has hardly begun, and already it feels unbearable.

It's as though you can't wait to get away from us.

His voice again. It won't leave me alone. Even two hundred miles from home won't be far enough today. Guilt at this thought twists my stomach into knots.

'Can you spare some change, please?'

The voice draws my gaze to a man wrapped in a filthy duvet, huddled next to the wall. His gaunt features and hollow eyes remind me of my brother. Without thinking, I hand him my coffee and croissant. His smile is startling, brimming with gratitude that feels out of place in this cold, indifferent concourse. I peel the cover from my phone, retrieving the emergency twenty-pound note tucked behind it.

'Here.' I thrust it at him.

'Are you sure?' His voice lifts, as though I've handed him a lifeline instead of what to me, is small change. For a fleeting moment, I feel lighter. But then the whispers return.

It's as though you can't wait to get away from us.

Stay away from him. Just bloody stay away.

Good luck – you're going to need it.

I squeeze my eyes together as if this can block it all out. Perhaps I *am* as bad as they all say. My head swoons so I quickly reopen my eyes. I'm woozy from not eating since yesterday morning but there's no time to fix that now.

'The next train to arrive at platform six will be the 7:02 service to London King's Cross.'

The announcement jars me back into the moment. I join the tide of passengers moving toward the platform as I fumble around on my phone to find my eTicket. The crowds feel thicker today, and they're pressing in on all sides of me. How can it be this busy so early in the morning? The thrill I used to feel at embarking on my weekly commute has gone and has been replaced by a suffocating loneliness. And I feel like people are looking at me – as if they can somehow sense what an awful person I am inside.

The ticket gate doesn't budge as I try to scan my barcode. A weary attendant smiles kindly, presses his card to the machine and waves me through. His small act of generosity feels oddly significant, a faint warmth against the chill of the morning. I've got to hang on to what I can.

I home in on the familiar face which dots the throng, trying to push my way through to it. Then I see one I really *don't* want to see so I backtrack, keeping my head down while I pretend to scroll through my phone. With a bit of luck, I'll blend into the crowd and not be noticed. Slip onto the train and pretend I'm reading. I can't take any more this morning.

'Back to the grind?' A voice asks.

I glance up, startled. A woman I vaguely know smiles at me. She works further down the South Bank.

'Um, yes. I guess so,' I mumble.

'Are you okay?'

'Why wouldn't I be?'

Her fingers brush my cheek, and I flinch. They're wet – tears

I didn't realise I'd shed. Embarrassment flushes through me, but the crowd surges forward, shoving us apart.

'The train shortly arriving at platform six will be the 7:02 service to London King's Cross. Please stand back from the edge.'

The robotic words feel distant, muffled by the buzz of voices and the chaos of movement. I should have eaten something – I really don't feel too good. A shout rings out, sharp and commanding:

'Stay back behind the line!'

But the crowd presses forward, heedless. My feet lose contact with the ground and I'm carried by the surge, weightless and powerless.

Then, abruptly, I'm alone.

Falling.

And the last things I see are the headlights of the oncoming train.

Find Out More on Amazon

INTERVIEW WITH THE AUTHOR

Q: Where do your ideas come from?

A: I'm no stranger to turbulent times, and these provide lots of raw material. People, places, situations, experiences – they're all great novel fodder!

Q: Why do you write psychological thrillers?

A: I'm intrigued why people can be most at risk from someone who should love them. Novels are a safe place to explore the worst of toxic relationships.

Q: Does that mean you're a dark person?

A: We thriller writers pour our darkness into stories, so we're the nicest people you could meet – it's those romance writers you should watch...

Q: What do readers say?

A: That I write gripping stories with unexpected twists, about people you could know and situations that could happen to anyone. So beware...

Q: What's the best thing about being a writer?

A: You lovely readers. I read all my reviews, and answer all emails and social media comments. Hearing from readers absolutely makes my day, whether it's via email or through social media.

Q: Who are you and where are you from?

A: A born 'n' bred Yorkshire lass, now officially in my early fifties. I have two grown up sons and a Sproodle called Molly. (Springer/Poodle!) The last decade has been the best: I've done an MA in Creative Writing, made writing my full time job, and found the happy-ever-after that doesn't exist in my writing - after marrying for the second time just before the pandemic.

Q: Do you have a newsletter I could join?

A: I certainly do. Go to www.mariafrankland.co.uk or click here through your eBook to join my awesome community of readers. When you do, I'll send you a free novella – 'The Brother in Law.'

ACKNOWLEDGMENTS

Thank you, as always, to my amazing husband, Michael. He's my first reader, and is vital with my editing process for each of my novels. His belief in me means more than I can say.

A special acknowledgement goes to my wonderful advance reader team, who took the time and trouble to read an advance copy of The Valentine and offer feedback. They are a vital part of my author business and I don't know what I would do without them. This is my twenty-first full-length novel and it becomes harder and harder to think of first names for my characters. Therefore, I'm really grateful to members of the group who offered their own names up for me to use! They are:

Tamara (Tam Gordon)

Dale (put forward by Connie Rosenbaum and Susie Smith Coburn)

Rachel (Rachel Fournier)

Sian (Sian Edwards Vaughan)

Jae (Jae Wheaton)

Ali (Ali Eaton)

Martin (Put forward by Claire Harrison Walker)

I will always be grateful to Leeds Trinity University and my MA in Creative Writing Tutors there, Martyn, Amina and Oz. My Masters degree in 2015 was the springboard into being able to write as a profession.

And thanks especially, to you, the reader. Thank you for taking the time to read this story. I really hope you enjoyed it.

Printed in Great Britain
by Amazon

57900369R00158